D0833341

Flight to Freedom

first

person

fiction

Flight

SCHOLASTIC INC.

New York Toronto London Auckland Sydney
Mexico City New Delhi Hong Kong Buenos Aires

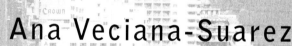

to Freedom

Ana Veciana-Suarez

Cover photo by Peter Guttman (www.peterguttman.com).
This photo has been digitally altered.

Cover design by Elizabeth B. Parisi.

Copyright © 2002 by Ana Veciana-Suarez.
Cover photograph copyright © 2002 by Peter Guttman.
All rights reserved. Published by Scholastic Inc.
Printed in the U.S.A.

ISBN 0-439-12392-5
(meets NASTA specifications)

SCHOLASTIC, READ 180, and associated logos and designs are
trademarks and/or registered trademarks of Scholastic Inc.

LEXILE is a registered trademark of MetaMetrics, Inc.

7 8 9 10   23   12 11 10 09 08

For my children, Renee, Leonardo,
Christopher, Benjamin, and Nicholas,
so they will always remember

Havana, Cuba

1967

Here we are, you and I, alone together. Forever. Or until these pages are filled with my handwriting. You are my first diary. Papi gave you to me this morning, before he left for the countryside. "For my studious daughter," he said. (That's me.) He had tears in his eyes when he said this, and his square chin quivered.

He gave Ileana, who, at sixteen, is three years older than I, a beautiful tortoiseshell compact with face powder, and for our younger sister, Ana María, a small rag doll with embroidered eyes and yarn for hair. I do not know if he got anything for Pepito because my brother was drafted into the army last fall. Our gifts are treasures in these rationed times, so I thanked him with many hugs and kisses. I did not want to cry in front of him because that would make him feel worse, so I tried to concentrate on his thick, black mustache.

Papi must work in the fields, harvesting coffee, so we can leave Cuba. The government assigns all the heads of households to *la agricultura* before a family can emigrate. Working the fields can be backbreaking toil under terrible conditions, especially for men like my father who are city folk and know nothing about farming. But what else can he do? Like everyone who requests permission to leave the country, he was fired from his job. We have had to depend on our savings and the generosity of family. Some do not even have that to fall back on. "All in all," Mami keeps reminding us, "we have been lucky."

We do not know exactly when we will be allowed to travel, but Papi has already been told that our exit permits and U.S. visas are being processed. When the paperwork is complete, we will board an airplane for Miami, to join my father's brother and his family. My paternal grandparents, Abuelo Tony and Abuela María, are there, too. We will be gone only a short time, Papi said, until the political situation improves here on the island. To prove she believes this, Mami had her long brown hair, which she liked to wear in a chignon, cut short like a boy's. She will grow it back only after we return. She has offered this as a sacrifice to Our Lady of Charity in hopes that our stay in the United States will not be long.

Ana Mari came home crying because other pupils in her school are calling her *gusana.* Everyone calls the Cuban exiles in Miami "worms," and since we will soon be going there, they insult us in that way, too. Those who know we have applied to leave the country think we are turncoats because we are abandoning the revolution and fleeing to the imperialist *yanquis* in the north. Papi says we must leave because the government has made indoctrination more important than the study of mathematics and grammar. Two years ago, when Ana Mari was entering kindergarten, the teacher asked her class if they believed God existed. Ana Mari and a few other students said yes, and were told to close their eyes and ask God for a piece of candy. When they opened their eyes, their hands were empty. Then the teacher asked them to close their eyes again and ask Fidel Castro, leader of the revolution, for candy. When they did, the teacher placed a piece of candy in each of the outstretched hands.

"There is no God," the teacher told the class. "There is only Fidel."

Oh, Papi was angry when he heard that! He got so

red in the face. I think that is when he decided we could not continue living here.

April is the anniversary of the Bay of Pigs battle, when a group of exiles, with the help of the United States, tried to attack Cuba but failed. In Ana Mari's first grade book, there is a poem titled "Girón" that talks about the invasion. "One time, in April," it says, "the Yankees attacked us. They sent a lot of bad people. They wanted to destroy the free Cuba. The people defeated them. Fidel led the fight."

We hear stories like this all the time in school, and my parents worry that the government is trying to poison our minds. Mami and Papi tell us not to believe everything we hear in the classroom because it is Communist propaganda. The only way to get away from this is to leave our home, yet I am scared. I am scared of a strange place, a strange language, a strange people. I am scared of leaving my friends behind, and my maternal grandparents, and my brother. When will we see them again?

Tío Camilo came into town from his farm in Matanzas and brought us all kinds of fresh fruit, a big ham, and a pork leg. Mami immediately hid whatever she could in the freezer and kissed and hugged her older brother as if he were one of the Three Kings bearing gifts on the Epiphany. In a way, I guess he is. It is impossible to find the food he brought us in any of the stores of the city. He also risked being thrown in jail for transporting these goods without government approval. But Tío Camilo doesn't seem to mind the danger. When Mami warned him to be careful, he told her, "Sister, under this government we must get approval to breathe. What am I to do? Suffocate?"

He complained that Fidel Castro had sworn to the people that his revolution was as Cuban as the palm trees. "Ha! Ha!" he laughed. "With all those Russians crawling around, no? This revolution is more like a guava fruit — green on the outside and red on the inside."

You would not believe what happened when I was waiting in line with Mami for our soap ration. She had heard from a neighbor, who heard it from her cousin's mother-in-law, that a shipment had arrived, so off we went at dawn. By the time we got there, there was already a long line, but we waited anyway. And waited. And waited. The day was hot and people were acting nasty. A fight broke out between two men ahead of us, but nobody tried to stop it because no one wanted to lose their place in line. Some people were cheering the tall skinny man, but I thought the fat, bald one was getting in more punches. As the men began to circle around each other, an old lady behind us screamed. It was a scream to make your hair stand on end.

Mami and I turned around and saw an old man in a yellow *guayabera* shirt lying on the street in a crumpled heap. The fat man and the skinny one stopped fighting, and people began to call out for a doctor. Finally a young woman broke through the ranks and identified herself as a medical worker in a lab. She bent over the man and pressed her fingers to his wrist. She said he was dead. We all sighed, but nobody moved. My mother's hands were shaking and her face was white. She ordered me to face the front and stop staring, but when she wasn't watching, I sneaked some peeks at the dead man. As the line moved, the people behind us simply stepped over him. Eventually two men in blue uniforms came with a stretcher and carried him away.

By the time it was our turn, the government store had already run out of soap. We wasted all that time, and now I cannot get the image of the dead man out of my mind. How horrible to die that way, without family or friends around you, waiting in line for some stupid rationed soap.

Monday, 10th of April

While waiting for the bus, Ileana spotted her best friend Carmen across the street. (Actually, I should write *former* best friend. They haven't talked in two or three years.) Ileana called to her and Carmen turned to look at us, but then continued on her way as if we didn't exist. Maybe she did not recognize who we were. But Ileana says she ignored us on purpose. Ileana and Carmen used to do everything together, so much so that Mami named them The Twins. But Carmen's father became a bigwig in the Communist Party, and he even has a car and a driver and is allowed to travel outside the island. So now Carmen refuses to speak to Ileana. She does not return her phone calls and ignores my sister as if she were a dead cockroach. Ileana does not blame Carmen. She is sure Carmen's parents prohibit her from socializing with our family because we are counterrevolutionary.

A lot of friends, neighbors, and even relatives do not get along anymore because the grown-ups argue about who is making the country's rules. After the husband of Mami's cousin Cynthia was executed by the *paredón* firing squad for trying to overthrow the government, Cynthia moved back to her parents' farm in Camaguey. Before she left, members of her neighborhood's Committee for the Defense of the Revolution threw tomatoes at her house, and she was fired from her secretarial job. I will never forget the pain and anger I saw in Cynthia's eyes on the day she left, the same look our old dog Mancha had when we found her after she was hit by an automobile.

I have already packed for La Escuela al Campo program in Pinar del Rio. My small suitcase bears my name: Yara García. We will be gone for forty-five days in this school-to-country program, but we are not allowed to take much — a few changes of clothes, a bucket for our baths, the standard wooden flip-flops, and a hat. In school we are told that the purpose of this special school is to educate students in agriculture and farmwork because they are important parts of the island's economy, but no one believes that line. Papi says it is just an excuse to obtain free farm labor.

Though I am finishing the seventh grade, this will be my first time at the country school. Last summer my parents were able to get a medical waiver because I had mononucleosis. Poor Ileana has never been excused. She has left home every year since she was twelve to help harvest the tobacco crop. She does not like to talk much about her experiences, except to say that it is hard work. We are supposed to attend school in the afternoon during this program, but Ileana says that rarely happens because there is too much to do in the fields and you work from dawn to nightfall, six days a week.

Mami worries about the bad influences I will encounter. I have no idea what she means and, quite honestly, I am a little excited about being away from home for the first time.

Saturday, 15th of April

My best friend Ofelia will be going to a different Escuela al Campo. She was heartbroken that we would not be together, but her parents have arranged for her to join the Communist Youth Union, and I think that may be why she will attend another program. We are all members of the Pioneers in school, and we are instructed to perform neighborhood watches to keep an eye on neighbors who might not be completely committed to the revolution. Most of my friends do not take this role very seriously because none of us cares too much about politics. We would rather play among ourselves or get together to listen to the radio. But when you are part of the Communist Youth Union, as Ofelia is, this is serious business. She will have to take part in conferences, marches, rallies, and undergo military training. I cannot imagine Ofelia doing this. She would prefer to dance or drink a tropical fruit juice with that Luis boy she likes so much, but I guess she has to do what her parents tell her to. Like the rest of us.

Monday, 17th of April

I must write quickly and without making noise. I do not want the teachers or the other girls to figure out that I am not really in need of this toilet except as a makeshift desk. Earlier today we arrived at La Escuela al Campo after a long, miserable, dusty bus ride. The boys took one bus, the girls another. Though a lot of the older girls were singing and carrying on, I was miserable and scared. The scenery, at least, was beautiful — green rolling hills and tall palms — and whenever we passed a *guajiro* leading his mule or oxen, we waved. The farmer would wave back.

A barbed-wire fence circles the compound. There's a row of small outhouses behind our dormitory, which is a long, crude building made of the woody part of palm fronds. When the wind blows, it whistles right through. (Sometimes the sound, high-pitched and off-key, reminds me of my grandmother singing one of her favorite songs, "Bésame Mucho" or

11

"El Manisero.") It gives me goosebumps, the wind's howling.

Thursday, 20th of April

The beds are deplorable. *Beds,* is that what I wrote? They are really pallets, burlap stretched between two logs, and there are dozens of them, each lined up no more than two feet from the other.

Because we are divided by age, I have not been able to speak to Ileana yet. She sleeps on the other side of the dormitory. I would crawl over there in the dark if I could, just to see a friendly face, even if only to hear her say, "Boba-bobita," which is what she likes to call me, but I am afraid to get caught.

Monday, 24th of April

We are awakened by the teachers before the rooster's crow, and we must get ready in ten minutes in the dim light of kerosene lamps. (It is like traveling back in time. Kerosene lamps, imagine!) A lot of the girls fumble and curse and yawn loudly while they dress. They even pass gas right there, without apology or embarrassment. There is no privacy or propriety here. It truly makes sharing a room with Ileana look like paradise. And to think I never appreciated it! Our breakfast consists of hard bread and strong coffee and occasionally slop that is impossible to identify. Oats, maybe. (Sometimes at night, I fall asleep thinking of my hot *café con leche* and toasted Cuban bread, slathered with butter — if my mother has been able to get butter and milk that month with her ration coupons, of course.)

Then we go to work in the fields or in the curing barns. Some of us have been assigned to stack the dried tobacco leaves in piles called *pilones*. We must do this in a rectangular compact mass, and then cover it with plantain leaves. I am not quite sure what Ileana does, but I think that because she is older, she must help in the harvesting. Morning is the best time of day in the barns, because it is not so hot and there is often a breeze. In the afternoons, it is sweltering and unbearable. Several girls have already fainted, but I refuse to give anybody the pleasure of seeing any weakness in me.

Most of the girls I already know from school, but we do not have much time to talk when we are working, and at night we are all too exhausted. I also remember what Mami told me: "Keep to yourself. Don't trust anyone." I talk mostly to a girl named Alina, but never for long and only of frivolous things. I feel sorry for her. She has terrible acne, and the other girls call her Granito.

Many other girls here are mean. They push and shove in line for meals. They make fun of each other. They claim that their father or mother is the head of the neighborhood's Committee for the Defense of the Revolution, or that the family belongs to the Communist Party. They expect to get privileges or respect this way, but it is all for show. Nobody wants to appear weak, and everybody wants to be more revolutionary than the next person. I feel sorry for us all.

Wednesday, 26th of April

I will spend six weeks here, and the thought of it makes me want to scream at the top of my lungs. How I will survive this I do not know, and so far from home, too. It reminds me of Pepito and how he must feel now that he has been drafted into the armed forces and is sleeping in a barrack full of strangers. My poor brother. How I wish I had been nicer to him.

A few days in this place, and already I sense I am becoming an ant, tiny and insignificant, one of many. So tonight, to keep my mind off my ant worker life, I have given myself one goal: I will not cry. No, no, I will not. This is what I have promised myself. God and Virgencita, Our Lady of Charity, please please help me.

Friday, 28th of April

Ileana was right. We rarely attend school in the afternoon. There is always some task to perform for the good of the revolution. Anyway, we went to school today, but it was a waste of time because all we did was read Fidel Castro's speeches. They are so long!

Sunday, 30th of April

Mami always tells me that if you concentrate on positive thoughts, you can keep yourself happy. It is so difficult to stay positive in this place, though. The only thing I know to do is to remind myself that my situation could be worse. For example, I know there has been talk among people in government about sending students to a country boarding school, where students work and study the entire school year, not just forty-five days. They would only be able to go home on a weekend pass. If the people in power decide to do this, it would be terrible for the children. The parents, too, because I know how my mother and father suffered when Pepito was drafted and when Ileana left for the country school in past years.

Wednesday, 3rd of May

We had a surprise inspection this afternoon. One of the teachers found you, my sweet friend. She opened you up, glanced through the pages, then threw you back onto my pallet. Phew! My whole body was shaking when this happened, but now I realize she probably could not read my handwriting without her glasses. My letters are tiny, and for good reason. I want to pack as much as I can onto the page.

I hate being fearful of everybody and everything. It makes me feel helpless.

Friday, 5th of May

Some of the crueler girls have nicknamed me Concen, short for *conceited*, and when I first heard it aloud, I felt like someone had punched me in the stomach. But I bit my lip hard so as not to cry in front of them. Now I do not care. They cannot touch me. They cannot hurt me. Their words are nothing, and I pretend that my heart is like a boulder, too hard and too heavy to turn. It feels like that anyway.

Saturday, 6th of May

Cannot write much. I have blisters on my hands.

Tuesday, 9th of May

Going to the bathroom last night to write, I ran into Hilda, the self-appointed spy of my group, Girls of the Vanguard.

"Why do you spend so much time in the bathroom every night?" she asked me.

"Use your imagination," I answered.

"What do you have in that bag?"

"None of your business."

She tried to grab it from under my arm, but I pinched and scratched her. She complained to Comrade Nilsa, but I explained that I had my menses, and that the bag contained sanitary napkins from home, a precious commodity here. I was not punished, but neither was Hilda. I hope she dies in the Zapata Swamp, attacked by a million mosquitoes and swallowed by quicksand.

Sunday, 14th of May

Mami came to visit and brought both Ileana and me a bag of canned meat she had bought in Havana's black market. I was so hungry that I wanted to eat it all at once, but she made us promise that we would pace ourselves for the remaining weeks.

Mami cried when she saw us. I wanted to, too, but I held back so as not to make her feel worse. She gave Ileana a long speech about being careful with the boys who work the fields and sleep in barracks on the other side of the camp. Usually Ileana rolls her eyes at a lecture, but she did not do that this time. I hear from other girls that there's a lot of hanky-panky going on among the older students, that the girls do not keep their curfew, and the teachers do not supervise them properly.

To be able to make the trip to see us, Mami had to show up for roll call at Havana's railroad station twice during the week to ensure she would not lose her seat on the Parents' Train. It left Havana at midnight and arrived early this morning in the nearby town of Ovas. She then had to walk along a sandy road from the station to the camp with the other parents. One of the girls told us that this journey is several kilometers, but Mami insisted it was just a short distance. I think she said that so we wouldn't worry.

I hated to see her go. So did Ileana. And you should have heard all the other girls crying when their parents left, too. The weeping was like the wind whistling through the wooden walls of our dormitory.

Tuesday, 16th of May

I have no energy left. We have been given a quota of work, but it has changed so many times in the past week that I cannot remember it. Besides, it is already obvious that nobody will be able to meet these figures. We are all city girls, unaccustomed to the labor of the fields. This fact does not seem to matter, however, and the labor supervisors have organized marathon workdays starting at dawn and lasting until 10 P.M. I am so tired I can barely pick up a pen.

Some of the girls want to strike. They say if we all stop at once, we can demand better food, fewer hours, and maybe even early release home. After all, we should not be treated as prisoners. We are supposed to be volunteers, these girls say. I agree with them, but I do not trust them. I think they are what my father calls *infiltrados,* spies. They are trying to trick us, trying to test our commitment to the revolution, before ratting on us. I will not fall for it.

Yet, I wish I could scream out how I really feel. Rub it in the face of Comrade Nilsa and Comrade Marta, who make us read Fidel's speeches aloud when we are exhausted, who taunt us if our parents are not members of the Party, who give us extra duties if we even smile at a counterrevolutionary joke. Right now I feel like a pressure cooker, ready to burst.

Friday, 19th of May

Is this hell? Surely it is, and somebody has forgotten to tell me. More later, when my arms do not hurt so much.

Saturday, 20th of May

Happy birthday to me! I am thirteen years old. Happy birthday to my country, too! Today is also Cuban Independence Day, which is why my parents named me Yara, for the *Grito de Yara*, though that happened not in May but on the tenth of October in 1868. On that day, we Cubans made a proclamation of independence from Spain. A ten-year war soon followed, but it was not successful. We truly did not break away from the Spanish until the turn of the century, and now we celebrate both in May and in October.

We had a program in the afternoon, parading around some flags and listening to speeches by the older students. One girl who looks like a donkey talked about our responsibilities to the revolution. Another spoke about how we are the New Man and the New Woman, the generation Cuban Independence hero José Martí dreamed about. Blah, blah,

blah. I was miserable. Nobody remembered my birthday. Not even Ileana. Well, maybe she did, but we were unable to talk.

Sunday, 21st of May

Though we were exhausted to the point of collapse, the teachers called a meeting tonight because they found antirevolutionary material among our possessions. Of course I immediately thought of you, my little book, my only consolation. My legs shook and my head pounded. But no, thank God, it had nothing to do with me or with anything I own.

One girl was discovered to have a Bible, and another had a gold-edged prayer card of Our Lady of Charity. Both things were confiscated, and the girls were given extra duties. After all those hours in the fields, they must now help clean the bathrooms. Outhouses, really. God save me from that. Those bathrooms smell putrid and at night they are full of toads and frogs.

I do not understand how this kind of punishment can be allowed. Who gave these comrades power? A government that made promises of democracy and freedom only to go back on them?

Tuesday, 23rd of May

I miss everything: my mother, my father, the tiled porch at my *abuelos'*, the fresh watermelon *batidos* on hot summer afternoons. I miss clean bathrooms. I miss my own clothes. I miss warm baths. I miss ice water. I miss having time by myself. I miss the feel of my palms when they were soft.

Sunday, 28th of May

Three more days. Three, three, three. A magical number. I am counting them down with such joy. Then again, three has never seemed such an immense amount. Now I understand the concept of infinity that our mathematics teachers have tried so hard to teach us.

Wednesday, 31st of May

Home! Home! We are headed for home. And you, dear friend, are returning with me — a little dirtier, a bit more frayed, but happy just the same.

Later

Mami took one look at me and burst into tears. "You have become a woman!" she said, but it did not sound as if she was happy about it. Ana Mari said my skin is as brown as a nut. She rubbed her little fingers on the calluses along the palms of my hands.

I am too tired to write. My bones seem to have liquefied.

Monday, 19th of June

I was told I would not be able to enroll in school next year because my family is planning to leave the country. "We do not want to waste resources on the useless," one of the lead teachers told me. Useless? I receive top marks in most of my subjects. That's what I wanted to tell her, but I had to bite my tongue as Mami has repeatedly ordered me to do. Besides, this news was not unexpected. It happens to many students. Marcos, our next-door neighbor, was kicked out of his last semester in high school because he refused to call his father, a Methodist minister, an antisocial scum in front of his classmates. I feel sorry for him because now he just hangs around the house and tries to do odd jobs. Marcos wanted to study dentistry, but because of his father's religious beliefs, he won't be able to.

Tuesday, 20th of June

We received a letter from Pepito. Actually, let me make a correction. We received an *envelope* addressed to my parents, José Calixto and Cecilia, in his handwriting, but it was open and empty. There must have been a letter in the envelope at some point, but it either fell out or the government censors kept it.

The empty envelope did nothing to lift Mami's spirits. Though I thought a letter — or in this case, a missing letter — could be considered good news because it must mean that Pepito felt strong enough to write it, it seems Mami thought otherwise. She insists that he must be in a dangerous situation, and therefore the government does not want us to read anything about his whereabouts. She tries to keep from crying, but the tears just roll down her face quietly. I wish Papi were here to console her. As it is, we have not heard from him since he left to work *la agricultura.*

Saturday, 1st of July

I walked over to Ofelia's, but she would not even open the door. "Scat!" she ordered. "I will get in trouble if my mother sees you." When she said that, my stomach turned. My eyes felt hot. I asked her again, but she would not answer any of my pleas. She has become a person I cannot recognize since she joined the Communist Youth. I can't believe she would give up on our friendship so easily.

Friday, 7th of July

Abuelo Pancho's face was the color of old ashes when he stopped by to tell us that Tío Camilo had been arrested for selling his farm products on the black market. Mami agreed to go with her father to the police station to find out more details, and now they have been gone for more than three hours. Ana Mari is whining that she is scared, and I do not know what to do with her. I'm scared, too. What if Mami is also jailed?

I wish Ileana would return. She sneaked out to her friend's house as soon as Mami and Abuelo went to the police, and we have not heard from her since.

Saturday, 8th of July

Because this was his first offense, Tío Camilo only had to pay a fine for selling his goods on the black market. He was also forced to spend the night in jail, though Mami and Abuelo Pancho tried everything they could to have him released. When he came to visit us this morning before returning to his farm, he looked like he had not slept at all. He was also very angry.

"I did nothing that was morally wrong," he bellowed. "These are *my* products from *my* farm worked by *my* hoe and *my* sweat."

Mami ran around closing the windows and shushing him for fear the neighbors would hear. Ileana and

Ana Mari giggled. I felt horrible for Tío Camilo, but also for us. It is terrible to have to be afraid of always making the wrong move or saying the wrong thing. We live in a jail with no bars.

Thursday, 13th of July

Mami got the news today that all our papers are in order and our visas approved. We will leave later next month, when Papi returns from *la agricultura*. She closed the windows, pulled down the shades, and turned up the radio before telling us. She does not want any of the neighbors to know, and she made each of us girls promise to not tell a single soul. Later she called her parents. She used the code we have all agreed upon when important information must be delivered personally: "Julio brought by two bags of ripe mangoes. Would you like some?" So after hearing about Julio and his mangoes, my *abuelitos* came over immediately, and they read all of the official papers with Mami. We hugged and cried, turned the radio louder. Ileana even danced a cha-cha.

Eventually Mami called a halt to the celebration, and she asked me to take dictation. She began listing the errands we need to get done to prepare for our departure. We are going to be very, very busy. On top of the list: Contacting Pepito. He must ask for a pass to come home to say good-bye.

I do not know whether to be excited or upset. I have decided that I should be both. One part of me is curious about what is on the other side of that wide, blue ocean. Will it be a wonderful place where I will make new friends and have a good time? Another part of me, though, is frightened. What if people are unfriendly? How will I understand what they are saying in English?

Wednesday, 26th of July

Today we had the big march around the plaza to commemorate Fidel Castro's attack on the Moncada Barracks, which gave start to the revolution back in 1953. (Funny to think it, but I was not even born then.) I did not want to go, but Maruja, who heads our neighborhood's Committee for the Defense of the Revolution, came to round us up. Mami does not want us to be singled out in any way, so we went to the march with long faces and heavy hearts. It was stuffy in the buses, and people were fainting right and left at the plaza from the horrendous heat. Do you think anybody cared? Of course not. All they want is for the masses to spill around the plaza so that journalists can see the millions supporting the Maximum Leader. What a joke!

There were tens of thousands of people participating in the march, workers bused from the factories, children from their day care wearing the red scarf of the Young Pioneers, and students just like us coming from their activities. Everyone was wearing the revolution's colors, red and black. When a man yelled instructions through a bullhorn, we obediently marched and cheered and shouted revolutionary slogans: "Fatherland or death, we will triumph!" And, *"¡Cuba, sí, Yanquis, no!"*

My throat is very sore from all the shouting. So is my heart. It feels as if it has been shredded by lies and deception, by having to fake belief in something I know is not true. I am also ashamed that I did not have the courage to refuse to march. How can I cheer for a government my family opposes, the same government that has sent my Papi to work the fields just because we disagree with its policies and want to leave? Why didn't I look that bossy Comrade Maruja in the eye and tell her what she could do with her Committee for the Defense of the Revolution?

Papi always tells us that the New Man the Communists want to create with their rules is really a social hypocrite who says one thing but believes another. That's how I feel. But then I hear my mother's warnings. I am not to do anything to make myself stand out. We must conform. We must keep silent. We are too close to what we want. To leaving. To freedom. Yet, I ask myself, at what price? I can feel this anger and resentment bubbling up inside me like *café* percolating.

Tuesday, 8th of August

Papi is finally home. Or maybe I should say that a man who looks like my father is home. He has lost a lot of weight and now he has gray hair. Mami teased him about it, but he didn't laugh. He didn't even seem happy that we had gotten our exit permits.

Saturday, 12th of August

It is ten o'clock in the evening, and Papi is still sitting out in the porch alone. When people come to visit, he leaves the room. If Mami or any of us speak to him, he answers yes or no but doesn't say much. What is wrong with him?

Tuesday, 15th of August

We will not be able to see Pepito before we leave. He is training in the mountains somewhere, and was refused permission to say good-bye to his *gusano* family before we leave for *yanqui* hell. That's how Papi told us, kind of making a joke of it. Then he did not say anything else, just went to his room and slammed the door.

Mami sat in the living room and cried with my grandparents. Ileana said we should write to Fidel Castro and ask him to let us see our brother. I would never have thought of such an idea, but that is how my sister thinks. Abuelo Pancho told her not to be ridiculous. They got into an argument, and I just came into the bedroom to get away.

All our stuff is packed. Well, not all. The government does not allow us to take anything of value, and the weight and number of suitcases are limited. I cannot bring most of my dresses and shoes, nor my pretty jewelry box. I suppose we will eventually get new ones, but I will miss some of the jewelry I have had for a long time, especially my baby earrings and the small gold identification bracelet I received for my fifth birthday. Those are things I can never replace.

Monday through Friday there are two flights a day taking Cubans to Miami. The airlift began in December 1965, when our government and the United States government agreed to allow people like us to leave the island. I have never been on an airplane before, so I am looking forward to my first time. Will it be a long flight? Where will we sit? (I would like a window seat.) Can we breathe so high up in the air, or will we have to wear a mask? Will we float as if we were in space? Should I take a *bocadito* to eat? Mami laughs when I ask her all these questions. She said it's like taking a bus in the air.

"You will always remember this airplane trip," she assures me.

Friday, 18th of August

We are in the air, flying. Though I have never been on an airplane, I am not afraid. It makes me think of Pepito because he used to say he wanted to be a pilot. I wonder if he is thinking of us just as I am thinking of him.

There are lots of clouds now, and it looks as if we are pushing through cotton. But when we first took off from the Varadero airport, it was a clear day. From the window seat beside Papi, I was able to see the green and brown of the island and then the deep blue of the ocean. Papi looked out, too, and he sighed. He said that now we were officially exiles. I asked what that meant exactly, and he replied that we belonged nowhere, not in Cuba and not in the United States. Maybe exile means staying forever in an airplane, suspended over an ocean between two countries, just like we are now.

A lot of people cried when the plane took off, my mother included. One old couple wailed and wailed. Even with my ears popping, I could hear them. They kept saying they were going to live their last years, then die, with strangers. I don't think either of them will die soon. Both seem very strong and plump.

In the row behind us there are two girls who are traveling alone. I think the oldest is my age, and they must be sisters because they have the same brown hair and cat-green eyes. There are envelopes pinned on their white blouses with their names in red ink. They have been holding hands the entire trip. If I were in their shoes, I would be shaking like a leaf. I would be scared to leave home on a plane alone. I wish I could talk to them, ask them why they are leaving, and whom they expect will meet them in Miami, but Papi told me not to stare.

My Papi. You should see his face. It is hard as stone. When he speaks, he barely moves his lips. I think he is trying very, very hard not to cry.

The pilot just made the announcement. We are landing soon!

Miami, Florida

Sunday, 20th of August

You must have thought I had forgotten you in some suitcase, but I had not. We have just been busy. All weekend, friends and family have come to visit, beginning in the morning and lasting through the evening. So many people, and I can't remember most of them. Some tell me that I have grown and changed. Others say I look the same. Grown-ups don't make any sense!

Today was especially busy. The family who used to live down the street from us in Cuba stopped by. They brought a sack of donated clothes from their church. Most were for Ana Mari, but I was able to fit into a pretty white blouse with lace on the collar and also a blue sweater, which I will use in winter. Ileana kept a square black purse.

Papi and Tío Pablo also met with their friends, and they argued about Cuba for hours in the living room. From what I heard, one side argued for an invasion, and the other side wanted people to rebel from within. Nobody seemed to agree, and after Abuela María offered the men coffee, she shook her head and whispered to me, "Talk and no action will never get anything accomplished." Then she tried to pat me on the head, but when she realized I am already taller than she is, she just patted my hand. In the kitchen, the women talked, too, but it was about children and what they needed in their new homes or about all the relatives still in Cuba. Everyone has left behind a parent or a brother or a child. One woman began to sob because her mother is dying and she cannot return to the island to see her. To me, that is very sad. A family should stay together always, at least until the children marry. Then the children should live close by.

We are staying in a three-bedroom house with Tío Pablo, who is my father's older brother. Papi and Tío Pablo look alike, with the same puppy-tail mustache, except my uncle is heavier and less serious. His wife is my Tía Carmen, who is short and very thin and laughs a lot. She thinks everything is funny. My cousin Efraín is seventeen, younger than Pepito and older than Ileana. He looks like his father, with the same big chest but without a mustache. He likes to joke around. The very first day we were here, he had a little noisemaking gadget hidden in his palm. When he shook our hands, it sounded like a gong. Even Papi was amused.

Also living in the house are Abuelo Tony and Abuela María, my father's parents. Abuelo Tony used to be my doctor when I was a baby, but now he can no longer practice pediatrics. Abuela María is soft and dimpled and seems permanently attached to my grandfather's side. Her hair is completely white, and she wears it in two braids pinned around her head. It's strange to hear her call my father by his full name, José Calixto. We had not seen any of them since they left in 1965, but they all look the same.

It is very crowded in the house. The adults have the bedrooms, and Ana Mari stays in a cot beside my parents. Efraín sleeps on a plain sofa in the back, in what they call a Florida room, right off the kitchen. Ileana and I share a sofa bed in the living room. It is lumpy and it creaks when we move. Ileana hogs the covers.

All Cubans must report to the Cuban Refugee Emergency Center when they arrive. El Refugio is a tall, tall building, probably nineteen or twenty floors, topped by a dome with slender towers. Papi said those are called minarets. The center stands across the street from the bay, and when the wind blows west, as it did while we were there, the sea mists your arms and legs. It reminded me a little of El Malecón, the old seawall at home, and I ended up getting a big lump in my throat.

El Refugio. The Refuge. What an appropriate name, because this place was full of people like us, refugees hoping to find jobs or places to live or locate relatives in the city. Some families were given coats and one-way airplane tickets to different towns if they did not know anybody in Miami. Mami and Papi had to fill out lots of papers and answer many questions. All the social workers spoke Spanish, and many were Cuban themselves. Because Papi does not have a job yet, the government gave him one hundred dollars and a coupon that allows us to pick up food at a warehouse. Tía Carmen said we can get powdered milk and powdered eggs, cheese, canned meat, flour, and other food staples there.

I wonder why a foreign government would give away money and food this way. Maybe this country has so much that it can afford to donate its extras. "It is more than that," Tía Carmen told me later. "The Americans are a generous people. This is a country built by immigrants and refugees, people like us who have arrived broke and brokenhearted, and then they have found refuge and comfort here." I guess that's where the name El Refugio comes from.

Wednesday, 23rd of August

Tía Carmen trimmed Mami's hair. Every strand that fell to the floor reminded me of something lost, something that I cannot get back. Does that make sense? It's as if Mami with long hair represents how our life used to be, how I would want it to be again, when I was younger and Papi was happier and Pepito was not in the army and all our relatives lived close by. Mami with short hair, on the other hand, is new and strange, different. I cannot get used to her in that style. She doesn't look like a mother at all.

We paid a short visit to Efraín at his job. He works at a store called Tandy Leather on a street named Flagler and sells craft kits to make fringe vests, headbands, and sandals. While we were at the store, Efraín waited on a customer. He had a long conversation with her in English, and we were all very impressed. We could tell he was proud of his English, too. Ileana now says she wants to get a job after school just like Efraín's. This way she can earn money to help the family while learning to speak English. Tía Carmen liked the idea, but Mami raised her eyebrows in that way she has when she thinks we are out of line. I think a job would be a good idea. If I were old enough, I would want one, too. I would like to have my own money, so I can spend it however I want to.

Efraín also introduced us to his boss, who does not speak any Spanish but knows how to say *buenos días* and *adiós*. He said his grandparents immigrated to New York from Germany and Austria many, many years ago. Later, while walking home, Mami told us that we are exiles, not immigrants. Big difference, she insisted. In what way? I asked. She explained that immigrants plan to stay in the new country while exiles live there only for a while. That reminded me of what Papi told me on the airplane, about being between two countries. Mami also said we are living a temporary life because as soon as the Communist government is thrown out, we will return to Cuba and resume our activities there.

"This will seem like a long vacation, that's all," she said.

Well, Efraín has been on vacation for two years then. And if it's a vacation, why do we have to go to school, find jobs, and fill out papers at El Refugio?

Friday, 25th of August

I wonder how my friends at home are doing. Do they still walk the three blocks to *la heladería*? (I miss the red mamey ice cream most. Of course, the shop did not always have milk or cream to make it. But when they did, it was so good!) Do they play jacks without me in Ofelia's house? Is Ofelia still participating in the Communist Youth? Has everyone, including Ofelia, stayed friends? If I remember too much, my chest hurts and my eyes burn.

Must go. Ileana is nagging me to turn off the light.

Sunday, 27th of August

We went to Crandon Park today and took a picnic lunch. We swam at the park's beach. It was so hot that the ocean felt like bathwater. Tío Pablo said this beach is on an island called Key Biscayne and many rich people vacation here. When Papi heard this, he made a funny noise in the back of his throat and said that those of us who are used to Cuba's beaches, like Varadero and Boca Ciega and Santa María del Mar, would have a difficult time adjusting to a mediocre place like this. I don't think that was a very nice thing to say, and Abuelo Tony told my father to enjoy what he has instead of pining away for what he doesn't.

We enjoyed playing in the ocean, though. We also ran into some of Efraín's friends from school. They showed us how to play a game called football with a brown pointy ball. Ileana liked this part best because the boys were making eyes at her. But then Papi told her to go back to our table and act like a serious young lady. She stomped back mad. In the afternoon Efraín showed us around the zoo. He bought us *granizados*. In English they are called snow cones. Those are the very first words I have learned on my own in English. *Snow cone.*

I forgot to wear a hat, and now my nose and cheeks are as red as a tomato.

Tuesday, 29th of August

Papi began work today at a hospital named Jackson Memorial. Tío Pablo works there, too. I asked Papi what his job was, but he waved me away angrily and said that it helps him feed the family and that is all I should care about it. That was so mean of him to say that. It's not my fault he's not happy about his job. Actually, he doesn't seem to be happy about anything.

Later, Mami told me he works as a bookkeeper.

Wednesday, 30th of August

Oh, the smell of *guayabas*! How it reminded me of home. Tía Carmen's cousin's house has two guava trees, and they are almost bent over with fruit. We collected as many as we could when we visited, and now their peculiar smell scents the entire house. All of us have commented on it. "Remember when," everyone says, and tells a story having to do with the fruit.

Friday, 1st of September

I am bored out of my mind. There is nothing to do except help Abuela María clean or cook. And we have done plenty of both. I have tried watching television, but I do not understand what is being said. Efraín has suggested I read some books, and he brought home some his boss gave him. They are about the adventures of a man named Doc Savage. I tried to make out the words, but it was too difficult. Mami says she will try to find me a few books in Spanish to entertain me. She also believes that once school starts, I will make new friends and feel better about staying in Miami. I hope she is right.

Tuesday, 5th of September

I hate it! I hate it! I hate it! I don't care what Mami says. I know I will never get used to this, and I know I will never ever ever like this school. How am I to understand anything the teacher says? English sounds like popcorn popping fast and hard on the stove.

"Patience, *hija*, patience," Mami says, but patience has brought me nothing but disappointment. Can't she understand? I do not know how to ask to go to the bathroom. I do not have any friends, and I do not expect to make any. I do not even know my way around the school, and twice today I went to the wrong classroom. (Ileana, who attends the second to last year of *bachillerato* at Miami Senior High, says she got lost going to each and every one of her classes, but there was always a boy to help her. Several speak Spanish. And one of the times she got lost, she discovered the bust of our José Martí in a courtyard. Imagine!)

I am in the eighth grade at Citrus Grove Junior High. Mami and Abuela María took me to the school this morning, but from tomorrow on I will take a yellow bus. The school seems enormous to me, with its big grassy field for physical education and long halls with dozens of classrooms on each side. It is nothing like my school at home. That was a two-hundred-year-old building with arched entranceways and wide porticoes. And until the government kicked them out in 1961, we had nuns who dressed like penguins. Citrus Grove houses three levels, or grades, as they call them here. I have a different teacher for each subject, but it does not matter because I do not understand what they are saying. Some look very young, and I was shocked to see one woman wearing a pantsuit. Slacks in public! In school! She teaches mathematics, and perhaps this class will be easy for me. We will be learning algebraic equations, and I have already studied that. Still, it won't be the same as home. Nothing can ever be.

At home I knew all the girls in class, and my teachers knew me. Here, I am nobody. Worse, in school I'm convinced I appear odd and out of place, like being the lone mango tree in a field of mameys. Mami made me comb my hair back in a ponytail like a little girl. Everyone else had hers in a flip. It was so embarrassing because I could feel my new classmates staring at me as if I were a visitor from outer space. Well, maybe I am, because that's how I feel. An alien who returned from one of those space trips with the Russian cosmonauts and is now pretending to be human. Ileana says I am making too much fuss over little things.

Everything else is strange, too. Here students do not stand next to their desk to speak. They simply raise their hands to be called on. In the mornings students put their hands over their hearts and recite something called the Pledge of Allegiance. I am to learn it by the end of the week, Srta. Reed informed me. There are also announcements over the loud-speakers and a moment of silence. But there are no official prayers whatsoever, just like when Fidel Castro came to power and abolished religion and all the penguin nuns left.

We do not go home for our midday meal, but eat in a large, noisy cafeteria. Today we had a carton of milk, a sticky white ball they said was rice, a strange green vegetable, an apple, and meat of some sort. But there is plenty of food, nothing like the rations of the last years at home. I tasted a little bit of everything, and I admit that it was not as bad as it looked. Still, how I missed Mami's cooking! Her ham croquettes, especially, which were always crispy outside but very hammy inside, and piping hot when I bit into them. My mouth waters just thinking of them. And how I wish I were back home in our kitchen with the blue tile countertop and the copper molds hanging on the wall! The cafeteria is so noisy, and no one, not one person, talked to me.

Later

Ileana says that if I truly am keeping a record of the family's journey into exile — *el exilio*, as Papi likes to call it — I should write that there is a boy in her American history class who looks just like Paul McCartney, the cute Beatle. It is already her favorite class.

And Ana María, little Ana Mari, dictates this message: She loves her teacher in the second year of what is called elementary school. The teacher's name is Srta. Blanco — Miss Blanco — and her great-grandfather was a Cuban who moved to Key West to roll cigars sometime in the last century. She gave Ana Mari a red lollipop.

I am the only one who is not excited about the first day of class. No friends, no understanding of what I'm supposed to do, no teacher I can talk to.

Wednesday, 6th of September

Can it get any worse? The social studies teacher, Mr. Peterson, asked a question in class and I had, of course, no idea what he was saying. Many of the other pupils raised their hands, but I just stared down at my desk. Obviously that was not the thing to do because he walked down the row to where I sat and tapped me on the shoulder. He said something. I looked around; I was so confused. Then I stood beside my desk because that is what I have been taught to do, to show respect, but everyone began to laugh. I do not know why. Was it the Spanish I mumbled? Or the way I stood next to the desk? Or is it this too big dress that my mother brought home from some give-aways at El Refugio? Whatever it was, the class laughed and laughed. I wanted the earth to swallow me. Just thinking about it makes me want to never return to school.

Though I am happy we do not have to worry about a bad government and the soldiers, I wish I could go home to Cuba, to the way things were. I want to sleep in my bed with the pink chenille bedspread. I want to listen to the tinkly music of my little jewelry box. I want to see all my old friends. I want to eat a big fat *papa rellena,* stuffed potato, in our very own kitchen. Most of all, I want to hear Pepito tell me to stop being a pest. *Sí,* most of all that.

I told Mami this. I told Papi, too. Mami said to be patient — she uses that word a lot — and her eyes got shiny with tears. Papi replied, "Soon, soon." How soon? Not soon enough, if you ask me.

Thursday, 7th of September

Tonight is the vigil of La Virgen de la Caridad del Cobre, Our Lady of Charity and Cuba's patron saint. Mami and Tía Carmen made an altar for her by setting two telephone books on a corner table and covering them with a flower-print sheet. Tía Carmen's statue is small compared to the one we had at home, but Tía Carmen says size does not matter, only faith does. They also bought red and white carnations and four votive candles at the tiny corner bodega and placed them around the altar. When we were setting up for the evening prayers, Mami and Tía Carmen warned us girls not to tell Papi how much the flowers or the candles cost. My Papi is always complaining that we must watch our money, that we are spending too much, that we have to be restricted in this and that, in everything. We are to pretend that these were gifts from the bodega owner, a nice Puerto Rican man whose wife is *americana*. Sometimes I want to put my hands over my head and pretend that I am in another life, in a world where I can have anything I want. Sacrifice and scrimp for what?

If I could, I would ask La Virgencita for a pair of fishnet stockings like the ones I saw the famous fashion model Twiggy wearing in a photograph. But Mami says we must pray not out of selfishness but out of compassion, kindness, and love for our families and the rest of mankind. But it is hard not to want what all the other girls already have! While the family prayed the rosary tonight, I could not help myself. Between the Hail Marys, I slipped in my own plea and then glanced around the circle to see if anybody had read my thoughts. Not one accusing stare, thank heavens.

After the rosary Mami did as she always does. She told us the story of how La Virgencita became our country's patron and protector. A very long time ago, sometime in the 1600s, the town of Barajagua needed salt, so they sent three townsmen across the Bay of Nipe to get some. A storm kept them at sea for three days, and the men prayed for rescue. When the storm finally passed, they spotted a statue floating in the water on a piece of wood. "I am our Lady of Charity" was the inscription on the wood. The statue was taken to the town of El Cobre, which gets its name from the copper mine there. This is also how La Virgencita got the last part of her name.

Tía Carmen says that the Cubans here in Miami celebrate a special mass for La Virgencita at the Marine Stadium by the bay. A boat brings the statue into the stadium and people wave their Cuban flags as she enters. This is a statue that was smuggled out of Cuba in a suitcase in 1961. I wish we had gone to the mass at the stadium, but Papi would not think of it because we have school tomorrow. (Another reason to hate school. I will always, always hate it.)

Because this is our first year in exile — "And our last," Papi assured us — Mami said our prayers would be different. We said an extra novena for Pepito, who we all miss terribly. Now every day that passes without him, I feel guilty for all the mean things I did to my older brother.

Our Holy Mother, Mami says, will intercede for him at the throne of God. She will also intercede for our country enslaved by the Communists. But when Mami tells us this, Papi gets furious. "Don't feed the girls such nonsense!" he shouts, and his face turns red. "We will free our country by taking up arms, by fighting." I agree with Papi. How do you beat a playground bully? Surely not by praying.

Four men nicely dressed in white linen *guayaberas* came to see Papi tonight. It is almost eleven o'clock and they're still in the living room. They are talking in low tones as if telling a big secret. I can tell Mami doesn't like what they are discussing because every time she returns from serving them water or *café*, her lips form a hard line and her eyes are narrowed into slits. Ileana and Efraín say the men are trying to convince Papi to join their political group, which is training to invade and liberate Cuba. They tried to recruit Tío Pablo, but Efraín says Tío has something called high blood pressure and he needs to be careful about what he does.

I wonder if Papi wants to train to be in this army. He was very upset when Pepito was drafted, but I know he wants to return home because that is all he talks about. Every one of his sentences begins with "When we return." Maybe an invasion is the solution.

I would like to go back, too. I miss my friends. I miss Pepito, and I also miss knowing where things are, like the pharmacy and the grocery and ice-cream shop. Here I am not allowed to walk anywhere. "You might get lost," Mami says.

Well, of course. And I'll continue to get lost if I do not learn where things are!

Though I am beginning to pick out a few words, most conversations I cannot understand. At night we can't listen to the radio too loud or laugh too much because the grown-ups are afraid the neighbors will complain about how many of us are living in one house. Being on my best behavior all the time can be tiring.

I wish the men would leave so that we can pull out the sofa bed. I am so sleepy.

By the way, I recited the Pledge of Allegiance perfectly in Srta. Reed's class yesterday. Of course, I had no idea what I was saying, but she handed me a piece of paper that said "Homework Pass." That means I can skip doing homework one day.

There are two girls in my science class who are Cuban, but both have been in Miami since their first or second year of school. They speak English well. Another boy, in my English class, arrived in December 1965, on the first Freedom Flight from La Habana. He said his photograph was published in the newspaper. I wonder if he told me that because I'm new and he thinks I'm gullible. There are other Cuban pupils in the school. I have seen them in the hall, and they all wear that same lost look of strangers.

Patricia, one of the Cuban girls, claims school will get better when I learn the language. On her first day of second grade, she peed in her pants because she did not know how to ask for the bathroom. Now she speaks English. She has friends. She also has new clothes — not a lot, but some. You can tell the Cubans who have just arrived, she says, by their clothes. They dress old. Old? "*Sí*, old," she said. They dress too formal, like they were in Cuba, the girls especially, with bows in their hair and bobby socks. And they wear the same thing over and over again.

When she was saying this, I fingered my hair bow, and I looked down at my socks. She was describing me to a tee, and my face felt red-hot. Mami makes us dress in nice clothes so that our teachers "receive a good impression." We do not have but two or three outfits of this kind, nice but old and worn. They are always clean even if Mami has to wash them by hand in the bathroom sink.

To be honest, at first I was mortified to find out how everybody regards me. Then I also was upset with Mami. She does not understand how school is different in the United States. But now that many hours have passed since my conversation with Patricia, something else, another feeling, has come over me. I am still angry, but at Patricia. At everybody else, too. I cannot quite explain why, but the thought of these classmates looking down at me makes me so, so angry.

I will show them. Just wait. I am going to be the best student in the class. I will get the highest qualifications of anybody. My marks will be outstanding. I will speak English so well, write it so eloquently, that no one will notice the clothes I wear. They will be mesmerized by my brilliance. Just wait.

Mami got a job. Yes, yes! Is that not something? Her very own job at a shoe factory. I am beaming like a flashlight. She begins Monday, and will be riding in a car with two other women: Lourdes, who is married to Tía Carmen's second cousin, and someone else I do not know. She is so excited. You should see her face, all smiles, and she has been humming since the afternoon. She has never had a job, not a real job outside the home.

"Now we can look for our own apartment," she told Ileana and me. "And I am going to learn to drive."

Oh, how I would love that. I love Tía Carmen and Tío Pablo, and Efraín is very nice, really, because he tells funny stories about his job, but we live like sardines packed in a can. We eat all our meals in shifts, and have to sit on the floor if everybody wants to watch the television together. And using the bathroom in the morning — that requires the speed of a sprinter.

I am so proud of my mother. So is Ileana, who says she is old enough for a job, too. I hope that when Mami receives the progress of my marks — they call it a report card here — she will be as proud.

It is terrible. Horrible. Worse than terrible. Mami and Papi had a big fight because of her new job. He does not want her to go to work. I think he is mad that she never consulted him when she went looking for work. Well, of course, she knew he would react this way. He was also especially angry when he found out that it is a man who drives the two women to the factory in this little town called Hialeah.

"What will people think?" Papi hissed. Yes, he hissed. That is exactly how it sounded. But Mami stood right up to him. ("Good for her," Ileana says. I agree.) She said she was doing something honest, and something good for the family, and she was very firm about it. But Papi told her she was absolutely not, under any condition, going on Monday. Her responsibility was to care for us.

"Who will be home when the girls arrive from school?" Papi asked.

"Your mother," Mami replied.

That got Papi mad at Abuela María because he said everybody had conspired behind his back, without any regard to his authority or our feelings. Tío Pablo pointed out that Tía Carmen worked, that there was no shame in it, but Papi pushed him aside, his own brother, and stormed out of the room, slamming the front door. We do not know where he is now, and it is very dark outside.

Ana Mari bawled so loud that Tía Carmen pulled her up onto her lap. Tía Carmen told us that we had to give our father time to get used to all the changes. "Change is always harder for men than for us women," she said. "They think they are *muy* macho, but the truth of the matter is that they are quite fragile. They also have farther to fall." I am not quite sure what she meant by that.

I wanted to cry, too, but I did not dare. It would just make things worse. I am glad for my mother because she took matters into her own hands. It is important, I think, to not just sit around and let things happen to you. But I feel badly for my poor father. How upsetting it must be to realize that everything you have ever believed in is not necessarily true, that everything you have worked for can be taken away by some stupid Communist government. He was always so proud that we lived in a nice house and that we had pretty clothes and that all his children went to private school. It must be difficult to give up on that.

Sunday, 17th of September

I'm not sure what happened between Mami and Papi, but it appears as though my father was convinced to give his approval of her job. A little while ago, she prepared her clothes and lunch just like a child preparing for the first day of school.

Monday, 18th of September

Tía Carmen and Mami enrolled in night classes at Miami Senior High, where Ileana attends school. They are going to learn English and will have homework just like we do! Mami told us not to tell Papi. I suppose that is because she thinks that would anger him. We already know what happened when she told him about the shoe factory. But I think she is willing to risk his anger. Today she came home so excited and inspired about having her own job that she immediately signed up for the class.

I hope they don't fight again.

Abuelo Tony told me an interesting thing tonight. After he heard me complaining about school, he took me to my uncle's bedroom and showed me a stack of books on the side of his bed. He said Tío Pablo was studying them all because he wants to be able to be a medical doctor in this country. Though he was a doctor at home, he still has to apply for a license here, which means he has to attend special classes and take an examination. Abuelo Tony said that if he were stronger and healthier, he would be accompanying Tío Pablo. "Your uncle never gives up, and for that I am very proud of him," Abuelo Tony said. When I told him that Papi thinks we will be home for Nochebuena, and if not Christmas Eve, certainly Three Kings' Day at the latest, Abuelo Tony shrugged.

"It never hurts to study," he said. "Nobody can take away what is between your ears."

Of course he told me this so that I can appreciate the privilege of attending school. That's what he called it, a privilege. I do plan to make good marks, so Abuelo Tony has no need to worry. That way I can show all those classmates, who look at me funny when I can't speak English, how smart I really am.

Tuesday, 26th of September

Today at dinner Ileana suddenly burst into tears. This came as a big surprise to us because she always seems so happy. Now we know that all along she has been hiding her sadness. After much sobbing and hiccuping, she finally told us why she was crying. She says she misses Pepito and worries about him, and that the meat and potato stew reminded her of our brother because it was his favorite dish. Of course that made Mami's chin quiver, and Abuela María began to recite a Hail Mary. Then Papi came around the table to hug Ileana. Her shoulders were shaking hard and her nose was running.

Poor Ileana! Poor Pepito! I wonder what my brother is doing. It has been so long since I heard his voice. I wish he would write, but maybe the Cuban government won't let him.

Wednesday, 27th of September

Mami is going to quit her English classes. It was either that or her job. I feel sorry for her because she was very excited about both. But Papi found out about the English classes when he came home early last night from his meeting with that military group. He blew his top when he couldn't find Mami, but he finally made Abuela María tell him where she was. Tío Pablo calmed him down, so when my mother and aunt returned, he was not too angry. I feel bad for my mother, but I also feel sorry for my father. They do not act as they used to. At home they hardly ever fought, and when they did, it was over soon and they would be kissy-kissy afterward. Now, after an argument, the air feels funny and thick. Even Ileana is afraid to open her mouth to say anything, and Ana Mari just sits in a corner hugging herself and shaking.

Friday, 29th of September

I think I have a new friend. Her name is Jane. The *J* in English is pronounced like a hard *G* in Spanish. She is in most of my classes and always talks to me when we are rushing down the halls to beat the bell. Today at lunch, just as I was ready to sit in my usual corner, she waved me over to her table. She is very smart and speaks very fast, so I have to listen very, very carefully to what she is saying. Now I understand a lot more English, but some conversations can be difficult. Srta.

Reed has told me that if I don't understand a word, I should just ask the person to repeat herself more slowly. I do sometimes, but I am embarrassed to do it with Jane. I don't want her to think I'm dumb.

Sunday, 1st of October

Papi has been out almost every night and all of this weekend now that he has decided to join that military group that plans to invade Cuba. This angers Mami, who mutters about his lack of responsibility. Abuela María tries to calm her down by telling her that it's just a phase, but this only gets Mami angrier. It's so tense in this house, I feel like I must tiptoe around everybody.

My parents can't even have a normal conversation. Whenever Mami says anything aloud about friends who have bought a little home along the Miami River or about her second cousin who has become engaged to a Texan living in Fort Worth, Papi shakes his head to deny it. He keeps saying we are living on borrowed time and on borrowed land.

Wednesday, 4th of October

We got four new Cuban students in our grade. Only one is in my homeroom, a boy named Pedro. He wears thick glasses and is very quiet. I tried to talk to him, but he seems shy. Jane said maybe he was just surprised that someone spoke to him in Spanish.

Friday, 6th of October

Two strange men in gray suits showed up at our door this afternoon. Except for Abuela, no adults were in the house. Since she doesn't speak a word of English, Ileana and I had to serve as translators as best we could, which meant we did a lot of finger pointing and head nodding. They wanted to speak to Papi, and left their business cards. Both are from a government agency called the Federal Bureau of Investigation. I'm not sure what that is — maybe a police agency of some sort — but it sure upset my parents. Actually, it upset Mami more than it did Papi. Mami told him, "This is a warning, José Calixto. I think you need to heed it." She was very flustered. I wonder what it all means.

Tuesday, 10th of October

Abuelo Tony brought home a bottle of *cidra* today. He popped the cork after dinner and ordered Abuela María to pour cider for each of us, even the children, so that we could toast. After she did that, he raised his glass and said in a booming voice, "To a free Cuba!" We drank. We celebrated for two reasons. First, because today marks El Grito de Yara, a national holiday at home because it is when Cubans declared their independence from Spain. More important than that, though, was yesterday's news that Che Guevara, one of Cuba's Communist leaders, was killed in Bolivia where he was trying to start a revolution. Abuela María said it served him right for going to a peaceful country and trying to make trouble.

"Maybe now we will be able to return home," Papi added.

I don't know how his death will translate into freedom for my country. Bolivia is very far away, in the middle of South America. It seems that sometimes my family wants so much to return home that they believe any little event, including this death in a faraway country, will make a difference. When I confided this to Efraín, he said I was becoming a cynic. I had no idea what that word meant, so he gave me a dictionary. It means a person who thinks everyone is motivated by selfish interests.

Am I really like that? I don't think so. I believe that people are good, that they try to do what they think is best. Of course, sometimes it seems as if nobody can agree on what is best.

I haven't had time to write much these past days because I have been studying extra long every night. When Efraín comes home from work, he helps Ileana and me with our school assignments. He is very patient.

Thursday, 12th of October

The World Series is finally over, and now our evenings will return to normal, without the men taking over the living room to watch and cheer during the games. Papi and Tío Pablo are big baseball fans. So is my grandfather. *Béisbol*, as we call it, is the most popular sport at home. I like it, too, both watching and playing. I guess that in a way that makes me a little more *americana* than I thought I was.

It was funny to watch the men, even Efraín, argue

about the strategy between the Saint Louis Cardinals and the Boston Red Sox. They were so serious! But they were having fun, too, and that made me happy because I hardly ever see my Papi enjoying himself.

Friday, 13th of October

Efraín showed me his Doc Savage books again, and I can read and understand almost everything. "Way to go, Cousin!" Efraín said, and patted me on the back.

Sunday, 15th of October

Through the walls I can hear my parents arguing. Again. So I cannot sleep. Sometimes I can make out the words, sometimes not. Mami is very upset because Papi left Friday after work, and we did not hear from him until he arrived home an hour ago. He returned dressed in camouflage, and as muddy as an alligator. He stank like swamp water, too. It's supposed to be a big secret that he is training with militia groups, but you would have to be blind and deaf to not realize what is happening.

Papi believes it is his duty as a Cuban to fight for

the liberation of his country. Mami screams that three little nobodies playing at soldiers in a swamp will do nothing against the might of the evil Soviet Union. She also thinks it is dangerous. Someone might get hurt or arrested. She insists that there is an American law prohibiting men from organizing their own armies to attack another country.

"Besides," Mami shouted, "if you do end up with your militia in Cuba, what are you going to do when you confront Pepito's regiment?"

I couldn't hear what Papi replied. If only *los americanos* would get involved. I wish they would send their soldiers and their helicopters and tanks and boats to my island, instead of far away across the globe in Asia. It makes a lot more sense to fight a war nearby. Plus, I think it would be easier to win on our little island. But nobody ever asks my opinion.

I have to go. The lamplight woke Ileana, who screamed at me. I hope she breaks out with a million pimples. That would serve her right.

Friday, 20th of October

Abuelo Tony has not been feeling well. Twice this week Abuela has taken him to a doctor. If the grown-ups know what is making him sick, they certainly aren't telling me. I asked Ileana and Efraín, and they don't know, either.

Saturday, 21st of October

The two men in gray suits came back. They took Papi with them and he was gone all day. Mami was hysterical. So was Abuela María. Both of them screamed at us over every little thing. They wouldn't even let us watch television or go outside to play.

We asked Tío Pablo what was going on, but he was too busy phoning everybody he knew to figure out how he could help Papi. When Efraín returned from work, he explained that the men in the suits were a kind of police, and they were probably questioning Papi about his involvement with the militia group he joined last month. Of course, that information only led us to more questions. Were they going to put him in jail? Would he be accused of a crime? Why had the national police taken my father? Papi finally showed up after dinner. Though he was pale, he assured the family that he had not been arrested or charged with anything, and that several men, also from his group, had been with him at an office downtown. He seemed to be trying too hard to calm us down, and that made me nervous. Mami refused to talk to him. Her face was red and her mouth remained pursed all evening.

Tuesday, 24th of October

Jane asked me to go to the movies with her this Saturday, but Mami said no, absolutely not. She said Jane is a stranger and we do not know anything about her family or her background. "We are not those kinds of people who let their daughters associate with just anybody," she said. What is that supposed to mean? Jane is not a stranger. She is my friend, and she helps me in school. She gets very good marks. I found out that her mother is a teacher in Ana Mari's school. She doesn't ever talk about her father, and I have never asked.

I think Mami was just in a bad mood because she found out that Ileana has been meeting a boy after school. He is a year older than she is, and he has a car and drives her home. She is supposed to take the bus and not accept rides from anybody, certainly not boys, but Ileana is Ileana. If you tell her to do something, she will try to do the opposite. My mother wanted her to promise she would not talk to the boy anymore, but Ileana refused. She told Mami that she is lucky the boy is her friend. He is very popular in school and plays football, that game with the pointy ball. She also said that they have done nothing but talk. He is very respectful and patient with her English. But Mami said that talk always leads to something else, and she wasn't going to have any daughter of hers tramping about without a chaperone. This got Ileana very mad and she shouted that we are living in the United States of America, not Cuba. So Mami screamed that Papi better never hear her say that. Then suddenly Mami looked around and spotted Ana Mari and me listening with our mouths open. She ordered us outside, and we missed the rest of the fight.

Later I asked Ileana what she was going to do. Her eyes were red from crying. She shrugged her shoulders. When I asked her the boy's name, she snapped at me and said it was none of my business. Then she cried some more.

I feel sorry for Ileana. I think she just wants to have

friends. She wants to be like everyone else in her school. I know the feeling. I don't think Mami or Papi understand what it is like to be new to a school, with funny clothes and a funny accent. They are not trying to be cruel to us. They may even think they are doing what is right. But it's hard to live like Papi wants us to live, suspended in the middle between two countries. We have to be either here or there. We have to make up our minds. We must choose.

Thursday, 26th of October

Pedro, the Cuban boy in my homeroom, is leaving for Los Angeles on Saturday. His father is a chemical engineer, whatever that is, and he got a job there. We looked on the globe in the classroom and were surprised it was almost halfway around the world. As soon as he saw this, poor Pedro turned white.

"I didn't know the United States was so big," he groaned.

"But look how close you are to Mexico!" I tried to console him.

He wouldn't answer, just hung his head. He wants to go back to Cuba.

Friday, 27th of October

Abuelo Tony turned seventy-four today. We had chocolate cake from a bakery and Coca-Cola. He was very tired, though, and he did not even bother to blow out his candles. I asked him what was wrong, and he put both his hands on his chest. "A man's heart can break in so many ways," he said. I gave him a big, big hug, and I think that made him feel better.

Tuesday, 31st of October

This is a day for the children to wear costumes and go house to house asking for candy. I dressed up as a Gypsy with Abuela María's clothes and a dozen plastic bracelets Tía Carmen bought at a small shop next to the Laundromat where she works. Mami drew a beauty mark on the left side of my mouth and colored blue circles around my eyes. Ana Mari went as a cat, with painted-on whiskers and nose. Her tail was a long black balloon. Abuelo Tony took photographs with his new camera. We collected so much candy that we cannot possibly eat it all without bursting. Efraín's boss sent us new toothbrushes. He told Efraín we would need them!

Just as we had planned at school, Jane and her mother stopped by during trick-or-treating, and Mami and Papi finally met my friend. Our mothers couldn't talk much to each other, but Mami invited Mrs. Henderson in. She made Cuban coffee, which Mrs. Henderson had never tasted. I'm not sure she liked it, but she was gracious enough to drink it. "This is very, very strong," she said, and smiled. Later Mami said that my friend — she called her *la americana* — and her mother seemed decent folk. Mrs. Henderson told her they attend Saint Michael's Church, so I think that made a good impression on Mami. Papi did not express an opinion either way, but at least he was polite and friendly and did not object to anything.

Friday, 3rd of November

I realized something today. I have not thought of my friends in Cuba in several days. I feel bad about that. Would a good friend forget so easily? I am curious about what happened with Ofelia and the Communist Youth. Is she enjoying it or are her parents forcing her to participate? Must she march in many rallies? Does she play with any of our other friends?

Papi always makes it a point to tell us a story about Cuba at dinner. Sometimes it's an event from history or a description of a historic site, but other times it is a story about the neighborhood or one of the businesses that we used to frequent. Tonight he told us about the José Martí House, in the southern section of Old Havana, and described the photographs and documents and furniture exhibited there. He could even remember the colors of the house — blue and yellow! He says we should never forget where we come from, so that when we return, it will be like slipping into old slippers found in the back of our closet. Memory, though, is like a piece of color cotton. Over time it fades.

I eat lunch with Jane every day. I have started packing my own food because I cannot get used to what is served in the cafeteria. Jane loves the croquettes Mami makes, but she does not care for the El Refugio meat. She says it tastes just like Spam. I like it very much. Now that my English is better, we also talk on the phone every afternoon. If Efraín is not around, she helps me with English and social studies homework. I help her in mathematics.

I have come to the conclusion that numbers are

the universal language. They count for the same amount no matter what country you are in. Yet you should see how *los americanos* do their division. They figure it out backward! They also do their subtraction very strangely. For example, they borrow by taking away from the top number. I learned by adding to the bottom number.

The American Way	The Way I Learned
$\overset{3}{\cancel{4}}\overset{1}{4}$	44
-29	$\overset{3}{\cancel{2}}9$
15	15

Either way, you arrive at the same answer, but if I try to do my calculations the English way, I feel like I'm turning my brain inside out. Mrs. Boatwright told me not to worry. She said several of her students do their arithmetic the way I do.

Tuesday, 7th of November

Jane gave me several books in a series about a girl detective named Nancy Drew. She read them three years ago, when she was in the fifth grade. These are much easier to read than the Doc Savage ones. Still, I read slowly to make sure I can understand completely what I'm reading. Sometimes I think Ana Mari will zoom ahead of me. That would be so-o-o embarrassing.

Friday, 10th of November

For homework I have to write a three-hundred-word essay about exploration in space because yesterday a Surveyor spacecraft landed on the moon. How in the world will I do that? I wish I were living on the moon!

Wednesday, 15th of November

Good news and not so good news: I received a perfect score on my mathematics test. Only one other person in my class, a boy named Derek, got the same grade. I am so proud of myself.

But on the essay I did not get a grade at all. Srta. Reed wrote, "Good try." Jane tells me not to worry about it, that I am too hard on myself. Yet I find English to be a confusing language, especially to write. In Spanish we rarely use the first-person pronoun to begin a sentence, but not so in English. I have to continuously remind myself to put the *I* when writing about what I am doing or thinking. When I read it back to myself, the composition makes me sound conceited with so many *I*'s sprinkled all over.

Thursday, 16th of November

Ileana is asking for trouble. She told Mami she was joining a sewing club at school but instead joined another club. Its name is Students for Peace. I am not sure what the members do, but I can tell you it has *nothing* to do with sewing. The only way I found out about this peace club is because the papers fell out of Ileana's notebook when we were moving our stuff to pull out the sofa bed this evening. It was a flyer in pink bubble letters and it said, STOP THE VIETNAM WAR. She grabbed it as soon as I saw it. At first she didn't want to tell me what it was. Then I told her I knew it had to do with that boy in the car, her friend who plays football, and she got so mad her lower lip jutted out as it usually does when she pouts. She pinched me, too, and said I was a busybody gossip, always watching everybody quietly and then scribbling in my diary. "Well, that's better than sneaking around," I shot right back. She called me a smarty-pants know-it-all and said that if I told Mami or Papi, I would have to sleep on the hard, cold floor the rest of my life. Then she turned off the light, and I had to go to the bathroom to write.

Friday, 17th of November

Ileana said she was sorry. I'm not sure if I should forgive her. I told her I would think about it.

Our marks came home today. I received an A, which is the top mark here, in mathematics. Also in science. I did not do as well in my other subjects, but I will not think about it because it will make me not want to try anymore.

Saturday, 18th of November

I miss Pepito, sometimes more than others. If I am busy with schoolwork, I do not think so much about him or about what our lives used to be like. I concentrate on the task. But on those days that I am home doing nothing but cleaning or setting the table or folding laundry, things that require no brainpower, my mind goes back to our old house and my other school, to my friends, but especially to Pepito. Is he lonely because we are not there? Is he angry at us? Does he think about us as much?

Sunday, 19th of November

When Papi returned tonight from his military training camp, he brought back a brown bag full of wrapped packages, one for each of us. I got a doll that looks a lot like one I left back in Cuba. This one is much smaller and prettier, though, with embroidery on the collar of her blouse. I like her, but the truth is that I am too old to play with dolls. In my room at home the dolls were more decoration than playthings. I would have rather received fishnet stockings. Or perfume. Of course I won't say this to Papi. It would hurt his feelings.

Ileana received a small bottle of perfume that smells just like the jasmine we had in our yard in Cuba. Ana Mari got a pink and white tea set. She wanted to set it up, but Mami said it was too late and we needed to go to bed pronto. Papi had a package for Mami, too, but she refused to open it. She kept her lips shut tight.

The weekends Papi goes away, Mami just mopes around the house and makes little comments about how she is going to raise her daughters not to depend on men. She says that in this country we will receive opportunities she never had, and good for us. Abuela María chuckles at this. "Man proposes and God disposes," Abuela mutters. I guess that means we can plan and plan, but it is up to God what really happens. If that's true, then it makes me not want to do anything. Why try so hard at school? Why work long hours like Papi and Tío Pablo? Why bother to train with the militia? It doesn't make sense. That's my opinion.

Monday, 20th of November

You wouldn't believe what I saw today when Mami sent me to the pharmacy to buy headache powder. First of all, Mami never ever sends me anywhere alone. She does not let me out of her sight. Even when Ana Mari and I play outside, we must stay in the backyard. So I was surprised that she gave me one dollar and told me to walk to the corner, then turn left, and walk another block to the pharmacy. I know exactly where the pharmacy is, but I listened to her directions to make her feel better. As I was returning home after buying the powder, I saw a blue car with big tires parked at the corner. Inside there were two people, and I was sure one of them was Ileana. So I stopped walking in that direction and hung around the sidewalk to watch. It was hard to see anything, but I inched closer, sticking next to the bushes, just like a spy. (I guess Ileana's right about me being a busybody!) From where I stood, I could hear Ileana's laughter. She has one of those contagious laughs that tinkle like choir bells. I could also hear voices and see silhouettes moving, but nothing else. I was at a bad angle, and the sun was shining in my eyes.

Because they were taking so long, I began to worry that Mami might wonder why I was delayed. Finally, just as I was deciding to backtrack and cut through an alleyway (which Mami has told me to never do because you don't know what lurks there), Ileana got out of the car. She leaned in through the passenger window and said something, then as she straightened up she threw her head back, and her hair fell like black waves. She looked like a movie star. That's when she saw me. She turned completely around to face me, and her jaw dropped. I'm not exaggerating, either. It dropped to the floor. I walked over to greet her, and she still couldn't get any words out of her mouth. I told her I thought she was supposed to take the public bus home after her "sewing club" meetings. She didn't reply to that except to ask me if I was going to tell. I said no, I wouldn't, but as we walked home, I asked her to tell me about her boyfriend.

His name is Tommy. He graduates from the high school this year and is planning to go to a town in the middle of this state to study at the university. I've never heard of that place, but it is spelled this way: Gainesville. He brings Ileana home every week after her so-called club meeting. (If our parents find out, she will be in big, *big* trouble.) She says he is very handsome and has blue eyes like that movie star, Paul Newman. He is a head taller than she is, so that means he is taller than Pepito. I don't know what they can possibly talk about since her English is worse than mine, but she insists they understand each other well enough. When she spoke, her voice rang out, like a song. That's how happy she sounded. I told her that she should invite Tommy to visit her at home, properly and with a chaperone, but she shook her head hard. She says I'm too young to understand.

What is there to understand? If she keeps sneaking around, someone's going to catch her. You don't have to be sixteen to figure that out.

Wednesday, 22nd of November

Patricia is not a nice girl. She never seems to have anything good to say about anybody. Today I did not have lunch with Jane because she was absent. She and her mother left early to drive to Tampa for tomorrow's holiday, when *los americanos* roast a big turkey and give thanks. After lunch, Patricia told me that I should be careful of girls like Jane. She says Americans call Cubans "spics" because they speak Spanish, and they also sing a song called "Row, Row, Row Your Boat" behind our backs. The boat-rowing song is sung in rounds, and it has something to do with the Cubans who float over in rafts. I don't believe Patricia. That sounds awfully mean, to make fun of people because of the way they come to this country.

Thursday, 23rd of November

This is the Thanksgiving holiday, on which we show our gratitude for all the good things God has given us. Tía Carmen seasoned the turkey last night and began roasting it very early this morning. She also made something called stuffing. The wife of the owner of the Laundromat showed her how to do all this last year. I had never eaten turkey, and do not like it much. It tastes like very dry chicken. Papi says that in Cuba turkey is called *guanajo*, and of course we all laughed until we had tears in our eyes because you call a person *guanajo* when he is silly and foolish. I did not like the stuffing either, but I very much enjoyed something called a sweet potato casserole that Efraín's boss sent home with him. It is similar to our *boniato*. So good!

We had black beans and rice, too, my favorite, and Abuela María baked a flan. Efraín said we should have had something called pumpkin pie because that is the typical dessert of this holiday. Tomorrow he will buy one and bring it home. So many different tastes! So many new things! I wish sometimes not everything was so new. It's nice to have old things, too — holidays and friends and places you know so well that they are already inside your heart. I like it when things are comfortable and familiar.

After dinner, Ana Mari told us the story of the first Thanksgiving. She learned it in school. Then she showed us drawings from her art class of the people called Pilgrims. It was very interesting.

Saturday, 25th of November

Big fight. Huge fight. Ileana wanted to go to a party, and Mami said that she could. That was two days ago. Then Papi found out and he said no, absolutely not, because he does not know the friend giving the party or her parents. Mami then convinced Papi that Ileana deserved to go because she is sixteen, seventeen in less than a month. Mami planned to go as a chaperone, but when Ileana found out about this, it was like someone had let all the chickens out of the coop. Even Abuelo Tony got into the argument, but I'm not sure which side he was on. That's how bad it was.

Ana Mari and I were told to play in the backyard, but we listened through the open windows as much as we could. In the end, Ileana did not go to the party. Tía Carmen said she was being hardheaded, which is true. Tía Carmen says that we must adjust to the new ways slowly, and we should let Papi do the same little by little. She suggested that Ileana take a chaperone for the first few parties. Then, as he gets used to new customs, Papi might allow her to go places with Efraín, who would be a good protector. But Ileana will not have anything to do with the idea. She said she would be the laughingstock of the school because nobody takes chaperones. That is not true because Patricia's older sister does, but I did not dare open my mouth. Ileana cried and cried. Her eyes were puffy like a frog's.

Tuesday, 28th of November

We are moving to our own house. Yes, yes, we are! We will be renting a two-bedroom house that is just around the corner from this one. I have not seen it, but Mami says it is well kept but small. Who cares? At least we won't be living like sardines anymore, taking turns at the dinner table and wiggling and jiggling when somebody is in the bathroom and we have to relieve ourselves.

I am very happy we will be moving, but I think I

will miss my uncle and aunt, and my grandfather and my grandmother. But I will especially miss watching television with Efraín. He has introduced us to shows like *Gomer Pyle* and *Bonanza* and *The Andy Griffith Show.* I especially like *The Flying Nun* because sometimes the characters say words in Spanish. In school the other students talk about these shows, and because I know what happens and who the characters are, I can participate. It makes me feel less strange.

Sunday, 3rd of December

We are all moved in. Our new house is a pale coral color, and it has pretty rose bushes that Abuelo Tony said will produce beautiful blooms if somebody takes care of them. I share a room with my sisters and sleep on the top bunk bed, Ana Mari at the bottom. Ileana gets her own bed and she has hogged up both nighttable drawers. At least we all have new bedspreads of yellow chenille. Tía Carmen bought them for us, for our good grades. I wish I had my jewelry box from home.

Mami spent the weekend scrubbing and scouring from top to bottom. We helped with our room and with the bathroom. Tonight she complained about her aching back, but I think she is happy to be here. She was humming along with Efraín's portable radio all day. We do not have a television set yet, but Mami says maybe the Three Kings will bring it for Los Reyes Magos on the sixth of January. She will have to convince Papi first because he insists we should keep our possessions to a minimum. "It will be easier to return to Cuba if we don't have to worry about too many belongings," he reminds us constantly.

Monday, 4th of December

Mami has a new boss at the shoe factory, and she is a Cuban lady who came over in 1960 with her husband and two sons. Mami says the new forelady did not know any English and had never worked before she arrived in this country, but she has managed to be promoted every few years and now runs the entire factory.

"Girls," Mami told us right before we went to bed, "there is a beautiful lesson in that story, and I hope you learn it."

Finally! We have received news from Pepito. My mother laughed hysterically when she found the letter at Tía Carmen's after she returned home from work. Then, even before opening it, she began to cry. Abuela María and Abuelo Tony tried to console her, but she would not stop. Actually, it was not crying but a wailing that pierced my ears. Ana Mari, who doesn't need any encouragement to break into her own tears, cried with Mami. And nobody had even read the letter! Tío Pablo was called, but he could not help. It was as if somebody had opened the door to a dam and all this grief could not stop pouring from my mother's eyes.

Eventually Tío Pablo was able to rescue the letter from Mami's grasp and he opened it and began to read it aloud. This seemed to calm her down. It was short and somewhat mysterious. "My dearest family," it began. Pepito, believe me, would never write anything so corny. He assured everyone that he remains in good health. He asked after his "little sisters who are so dear and precious." This is Pepito writing?

He did not mention anything about his military service, not even where he is stationed. He also did not say anything about the increased food rationing, but he wrote about the birth of a baby to one of our cousins and about my Abuelo Pancho's rheumatoid arthritis, for which he is being treated free of charge — Tío Pablo snorted loudly when he read this — at a state-run clinic.

When Papi arrived from work, the letter was reread aloud. Twice, in fact, and both times everyone kept trying to dissect and analyze each line for hidden meanings that might have escaped the government censors. My mother was inconsolable during every reading. Yesterday my brother turned nineteen. Alone. Far from us. As a conscripted *miliciano*.

There was other important news, too, which Tío Pablo read to us from the newspaper. The world's first successful heart transplant was conducted in South Africa by a doctor named Christiaan Barnard. Abuela María said, "What will they think of next!"

All night I have thought of the man with the transplanted heart. And *sí*, I will admit that I cried, but just a bit and very quietly. The man with the transplant is just like me — or should I say, I am just like him. My heart, the one now beating in my chest, feels like it belongs to someone else. It has been transplanted here, and everybody seems to want to force it to feel something it cannot feel. I may know a little more English, and I may now have a friend or two, but I do not belong here, in this country with street signs I do not always understand and people who do not understand me.

Friday, 8th of December

Jane got in trouble at school because of something another girl said about me. It was so unfair. Jane now has to complete an extra page of mathematics homework. We were working quietly when Claudia — that's the girl's name — said that it was a good thing I got good grades in class because I sure didn't know how to dress. I was so upset by this remark that I didn't know how to reply, but Jane said it was a good thing Claudia had a quick tongue because that way she could keep her buckteeth inside her mouth. Claudia then shouted something I did not understand, and Jane called her a stupid hillbilly. That's when Mrs. Boatwright came into the class. She had been outside talking to another teacher and only heard what Jane said, not a word by Claudia. I wanted to talk to Mrs. Boatwright after class, but Jane wouldn't let me. She said that if I did, the other pupils would think I was a tattletale.

Speaking of tattletales. Tonight, after everyone was asleep, Ileana woke me up and asked me to sneak out with her to meet Tommy because she was scared of going alone. I couldn't believe my ears, and of course I went. Though it was past 11 P.M., we met him at the corner and took a ride to the airport to watch the planes land and take off. Tommy and Ileana kissed in the backseat while I sat in the front, very bored and very nervous. Finally I turned around and told them we needed to return home. Tommy was not happy.

"Your sister needs a boyfriend," he told Ileana.

I wouldn't dare.

Saturday, 9th of December

Today we traveled downtown on a public bus. I was very sleepy from being out late, but the streets were decorated for Christmas, with silver bells on light poles and red garland draped over storefronts, so I paid attention. On one corner there was even a man dressed up as Santa Claus with a red kettle. He was sweating in the outfit because it was so hot.

Tía Carmen showed us this very fancy store that she says is similar to the old El Encanto back home. This fancy store in Miami is called Burdines, and it is very big. The salesladies were nice and they let us spray perfume on our wrists. Mami and Tía Carmen tried on clothes, too, and they giggled when they posed with the new outfits in front of the dressing room mirrors. Of course we did not buy anything. We had our noon meal at Walgreen's, which has a lunch counter like the *tencens* we had in Cuba. I tried a dish called a grilled cheese. It was delicious!

Later, after Efraín arrived from work, we watched television to see the daughter of President Johnson get married in the big mansion where the president lives. Her dress was beautiful, with a long train and puffy veil. Ileana said that when she gets married, she wants to wear a short red dress, something no one has ever thought of wearing to a wedding. I plan to have a long, white dress with lots of pearls stitched on the bodice, and the train will be so long that I will need six flower girls, three on each side, to carry it down the church aisle. Papi laughed when I said this, but when I looked closely at his face to see if he was making fun of me, I was surprised to find tears in his eyes. Then he said very softly, "I suppose you will want to get married in Los Pasionistas." That is the church in our old neighborhood in Cuba, but I was actually thinking of Saint Michael's, our new church. I didn't say anything, but I wish Papi would stop making comments like that. It makes me feel uncomfortable. I don't know exactly why. Maybe it is because I feel he should not worry so much about what is behind and think instead of what is ahead. Sometimes when Papi says certain things aloud, Tío Pablo tells him it won't do him any good to live in the past. It is the exile's curse, my uncle says, to always be looking over your shoulder.

Sunday, 10th of December

I have a secret! Tía Carmen and Efraín are teaching Mami to drive. They made me promise to not tell, and I won't. Never. Not even Ileana knows. Of course I don't know what Mami will drive. We do not have a car.

Besides, she needs a lot of practice. She drives around the neighborhood only for a couple hours while Papi is training with his militia group. She always makes sure she's home before he gets back.

Tuesday, 12th of December

Abuelo Tony was taken to the hospital today. There is something wrong with his heart, and doctors must do something to it to make it better. I asked if that meant he was getting a new heart, like that man we read about in the newspaper, but Abuela María said no. He gets to keep his own, with some fixes. I am worried about him. He looked so pale before he left and he seemed to be out of breath all the time.

I wonder how my brother is feeling. Is he doing anything dangerous in the army or is he working in an office, comfortable and safe? I know he is Mami's biggest worry. The other night I heard her tell Tía Carmen that sometimes she feels as if she abandoned her son in Cuba. Tía Carmen told her not to think such foolish thoughts. Mami had to leave with the rest of the family because the Freedom Flights are a once-in-a-lifetime opportunity. Soon Pepito will join us, my aunt insisted. I hope so. I love my brother more now that he is far away. I think it is true what grown-ups say about distance making the heart grow fonder.

Thursday, 14th of December

I am so proud. Today when we went to visit Abuelo at the hospital, I served as a translator for Mami. I understood everything the nurses and volunteers at the information center told me. Mami was impressed, too. I had already noticed I was improving my English because I just zip through the Nancy Drew books. I am ready for something more difficult.

You have to be sixteen years old to visit the patient rooms, but I snuck in with Mami. Abuelo did not look well. He seemed to have shrunk, and he was all wrinkled. He slept during our entire visit. I am worried about him. Maybe he does need a new heart.

Saturday, 16th of December

Ileana wanted me to sneak out with her again tonight. She said a whole group of students from her school are planning to have their own Christmas party at a construction site and maybe I would meet a boy I liked. She says I look old enough to be a ninth or tenth grader. I wouldn't go, though. What if we get caught? But now I'm sorry I didn't. It is almost midnight, and she is not back. If I had gone, she probably would've returned by now.

Monday, 18th of December

Today Tommy came to the house with another girl. He pretended that he had never met me. The three of them worked on a school project about the thirteen American colonies. Ileana draws well, so on a piece of poster board she sketched a farm scene from a book Tommy borrowed from the library. He was very nice. And, in daylight, I could also tell he was handsome. His hair is long, but not as long as some of those rock 'n' roll singers like John Lennon or Mick Jagger. I could tell Mami liked him despite the hair because he was very polite and said, "yes, ma'am" and "no, ma'am." Of course, neither of them knew what the other was saying. Ileana had to translate for both Mami and Tommy during the entire visit. Because of the guests, we were allowed to drink Coca-Cola and eat the guava pastries Mami bought just for Ileana's friends. They left before Papi arrived from work. Mami made sure of that.

Every night Ana Mari practices Christmas songs she is learning for a winter festival at school. I recognize most of the melodies, but the words are different. She sings "Jingle Bells" and "Silent Night," both of which I know only in Spanish. When she does this, I get a lump in my throat thinking of past holidays and of Pepito spending this year's alone. He probably will not be allowed to visit my grandparents, and for years there has been talk by the Communist government about outlawing the festivities. The talk, though, never did dampen our neighborhood's enthusiasm for the holiday. We always managed to celebrate in some way even when the rationing was bad. Cousins would stop by, and we would listen to Mami's long-play records of *villancicos* caroling away. Mami would set up, in a corner of the living room, the old Nativity set she inherited from a great-aunt. And Mami's oldest brother, Tío Camilo, always managed to bring us a *lechón* or, at the very least, a pork leg from his farm for Nochebuena.

Here we do not have any decorations except for some drawings Ana Mari made in school with construction paper and crayons. Efraín's boss gave him a Christmas tree, and Tía Carmen has decorated it with garlands and glass balls she bought at sales in a discount store named Zayre. I wish we had a tree, too — a silver one with blue balls. I suggested it once, but Papi immediately dismissed the idea. He considers it a waste of money. I wish he would change his mind.

Wednesday, 20th of December

Abuelo Tony is back from the hospital. He looks better but much skinnier.

Friday, 22nd of December

We had a big surprise at Ana Mari's school during the winter festival when she and four other girls sang two Christmas songs in Spanish. One of the carols is a lovely melody we used to sing in church when I was very little. Although I have forgotten its name, I can't help but hum it as I write: *Vamos, pastores, vamos, a la gloria de Edén. Vamos a Belén a ver ese niño.* "Let us go, shepherds, let us go to the glory of Eden. Let us go to Bethlehem to see the child."

When they heard this, lots of people in the school cafeteria got to their feet and clapped with delight. Some of the women cried. I suppose the carols reminded them of home. One man shouted, "¡Viva Cuba libre!" And Papi said, "Bravo! Bravo!" I was so glad to see him happy. But for me it was strange, because those songs come from another world. They belong in another life. They should be performed not in a cafeteria but in the arched entranceway of my old school. And they should be followed not by chocolate chip cookies and punch but by *turrones*. (I like the almond nougats best.) It seems as if everything is being thrown together all at once, one world blending into the other. It's hard to keep them apart. Jane thinks this is good, but she doesn't understand how confusing it can be. Just because my parents eat chocolate chip cookies doesn't mean they will let Ileana attend a party without a chaperone. And because everybody is trying to sing along to the words of a carol in Spanish doesn't mean the Claudias of the world will stop teasing us about our accents or our clothes.

Sunday, 24th of December

Nochebuena. The smell of roasting pork fills the house. It is the best smell in the world. Mmmm! Tonight the entire family will gather here to celebrate Christmas Eve. I have invited Jane and Mrs. Henderson, too. At first we were going to have the celebration at Tío Pablo's, but Abuela María had the idea of moving it here, to the backyard where we will all fit around a long folding table Efraín's boss lent him. Since we are making the pork, Tía Carmen is making the black beans and rice and the yucca. I'm hungry just thinking about it. But it also makes me sad because it reminds me of home and of all the cousins who would visit for Nochebuena, bringing a flan or a *turron,* or some cider or rum. At midnight we would all go to mass, even the children, and I would fall asleep on my mother's lap. What are my cousins doing now? Is Pepito home with Mami's parents? Are they able to eat pork? Mami and Papi have been trying to place a phone call to Cuba, but it is almost impossible to do so. There are very few phone lines, and a long distance call is very expensive. Sometimes it takes days just to be able to reach someone on the island, and that is if you're lucky and your relative is at home when the operator finally puts the call through.

Later

I am so full! It was a wonderful night. Jane and Mrs. Henderson had a good time. I could tell because Mrs. Henderson laughed at Tío Pablo's stories and helped us women with the washing and the cleaning. She brought a pastry she made herself, something called an apple pie, and it was very tasty. She put vanilla ice cream on top of the warm pastry. O-o-oh! Efraín had three pieces.

Mrs. Henderson also told my parents that I was invited to a dance party she and Jane will host at her house for New Year's Eve. She is asking ten girls and ten boys, and several parents will be present — including mine, if they would like to. Papi smiled at her politely but told her I was much too young to go to any party, especially on that night, when tradition calls for Cuban families to remain together. Mrs. Henderson blushed, and I was mortified, but thank goodness Papi at least told her we were honored at the invitation.

I'm leaving the best for last. Jane gave me the most

fantastic gift. (Here families exchange presents not on Three Kings' Day, as we do, but on Christmas.) Anyway, guess what she gave me? Fishnet stockings! It is the most beautiful gift in the world. I am wearing them to midnight mass. I have to think of a good gift for her from Los Reyes Magos. Efraín says he will lend me the money if I help him cut the grass at his house.

Must go. Mami is calling me to church. I know I will not fall asleep tonight.

Wednesday, 27th of December

From happiness to sadness so quickly. Mami has been crying almost every night. And when she is not crying, she sits alone staring into space. Ana Mari sits on her lap and hugs her, but she doesn't pay much attention to the hugs. I also show her all the Nancy Drew books I am reading while on school vacation, but she just nods and looks away. She misses Pepito very much and has not stopped talking about him this week. Tía Carmen says that everybody gets depressed during the first holidays in exile. She remembers she could barely get out of bed, and if not for her job, she would have buried herself under the covers.

Ileana does not help matters, either. Tonight she had a fight with Papi because he will not let her go out with friends to see a movie on Friday. He said a nice young lady from a decent family spends the holidays at home with her loved ones, not tramping about the city. (I think he does not want her to fall in love with a boy if we are to return home soon.) But she screamed that this outing was for only one night. Since she wasn't allowed to go, she has locked herself in the room. We are not allowed in. Whenever she has a fight with Mami or Papi, Ana Mari and I pay for it. If I wanted to, I could get Ileana in lots more trouble. Not only does she sneak out every once in a while, but I also know that every morning during Christmas vacation, between the time Mami leaves for work and Abuela María comes to take care of us, Ileana has talked on the phone to Tommy. She is lucky I am not a tattletale.

Sunday, 31st of December

I am so sleepy I can barely write, but I am determined to stay up until midnight so that I can eat the traditional twelve grapes that will bring luck and prosperity for the new year. Abuelo Tony slept all afternoon just so he can be the one to throw the bucketful of water out the front door. This will wash away the old year and everything we do not want to keep. Papi says we need a lot of washing away. Lots of buckets. An entire bucket brigade. Sometimes my father can be very funny.

I wish I could have gone to Jane's party. Ileana even suggested I sneak out, but I'm not as brave as she is. Right now I'm going to concentrate on figuring out what to give Jane for Los Reyes Magos. It has to be something special but not too expensive.

1968

Thursday, 4th of January

1968. 1968. This is the first time I write out each of the digits in the new year. How strange the eight feels. Like an exile!

Tía Carmen took us three girls for a haircut. We did not go to a beauty salon as we used to at home but to my aunt's hairdresser, who now gives her old clients a trim or a permanent in her own living room. Tía Carmen says her dentist and her doctor from Cuba also see patients in their homes. Like Tío Pablo, each is studying to get a license here, but in the meantime they help their old patients and charge them whatever the patients can afford. Ileana, who is very smart when she is not arguing with our parents, said this kind of arrangement is called an underground economy, which means that people work without the government knowing about it. She also said that more and more people will begin to do this because the government is too busy with the war to serve its people right. This does not sound like Ileana at all, and I am sure she is repeating what Tommy tells her. Tía Carmen told her to stop being a party pooper and be grateful for what she has.

I got my hair cut short just like Mami's. Though I wish Mami would grow her hair back, I like my new cut very much. It makes me look older and more serious. I think I look a little like the movie star Audrey Hepburn. Won't Jane be surprised to see me! After our haircuts, Tía Carmen took us to G. C. Murphy's, and she and Ileana helped me pick out a gift for Jane. I bought a 45 record of Aretha Franklin singing "Respect." Jane sings that song a lot. It makes me want to dance.

Saturday, 6th of January

Jane loved the gift. We do not have a record player, so we could not listen to it, but she said that as soon as she got home, she would play it on her mom's.

Her grandparents, who are visiting for the holidays, brought her to the house, but only for a little while. They are very old, older even than mine. They have white hair and blue eyes the color of the sky and both dress the same, like twins, in blue jeans and in cowboy shirts. Every summer they take Jane on a car trip, and they want me to come along when school's out. Wouldn't that be fantastic? I would do anything to be allowed to go. Maybe I can start working on Papi now!

Jane's grandparents were surprised I was not a Negro. They said they thought all the people from the Caribbean islands were Negro. I explained that many are, but my great-grandparents came from Spain. This got me thinking about how people from different countries really do not know much about each other. When I first got here, I thought all *los americanos* would be very tall and blond. I thought they would eat only hamburgers. But I discovered that is not true. Like Cubans, *americanos* come in all sizes and colors. They eat different foods, and the language sounds different depending on who is speaking. Mr. Fixx, the physical education teacher, has an accent that Jane says comes from the South. He sounds very different from Jane's grandparents, who lived in a place called Pittsburgh until they retired.

For Three Kings' Day, I received a new lime-colored dress from Mami and Papi. It is to be worn only for church or special occasions. Tía Carmen and

Tío Pablo got me a very pretty blue pant-skirt (just like the ones everyone at school is wearing) and a matching blouse. From Abuela and Abuelo, I received talcum powder and a bottle of an Avon perfume called Sweet Honesty. It smells wonderful. Abuelo Tony then teased me about being so pretty and smelling so good that all the boys would fall at my feet. If he only knew that they do not even know I exist. Besides, all of them are so short, and they act so silly.

Monday, 8th of January

I wore my new pant-skirt to school. I also put a little perfume behind my ears, in the same way Ileana and Mami like to do. With my new haircut, everyone thought I was a new student. Even Srta. Reed said I looked like — guess who — Audrey Hepburn! Julio and David sat with us at lunch and told jokes. Both kept looking at me as if they had never seen me before. Now I know how Ileana feels when boys turn around to look at her. She is very pretty and she knows it, but now I can look pretty, too. I was walking in the clouds all day.

I felt so good I decided to ask Papi about the car

trip with Jane. "Are you crazy?" he shouted at me, then walked away. He wouldn't even discuss it! I guess I have my work cut out for me.

Friday, 12th of January

Abuelo Tony is back in the hospital. I think he is very sick, but no one tells us children about why he is there. Please, dear God, take care of my *abuelito*. I love him so much.

Saturday, 13th of January

I thought of my friend Ofelia in Cuba a lot today. When I was home, I used to walk down the block to her house almost every day, and together we would listen to the radio and pretend we were singing into a microphone. We would dance with each other, too, trying to learn new steps, and if one of us stepped on the other's toes, we would collapse in a chair, laughing. Can we remain friends even if our families do not agree on politics? Will I ever see her again?

Papi insists we won't be here long. On New Year's Day, when we went to Tío Pablo's after mass, he said,

"*Año Nuevo en La Habana.*" Well, it is thirteen days into the New Year, and we are not in Havana at all. When we do return, I would like to come visit Miami. I am beginning to like it here. I know the teachers and they know me. I have friends. I have even grown used to the language.

Besides, we got a black-and-white television set from Efraín's boss because Mr. F.'s family bought a new one. Now we don't have to go to my uncle's house to watch our shows.

Tuesday, 16th of January

The call finally went through to Cuba. It was late last night, but Mami woke everyone up so that we could talk to my grandparents. They sounded as if they were talking through water. I didn't get to say much except "I love you." Pepito was not there. No one knows where he is stationed now, and this worries Mami even more.

Papi says Abuelo Tony is getting better, but if he truly is, why can't I visit him at the hospital?

Thursday, 18th of January

Ileana gets home about an hour late each afternoon. I am sure she is not taking the school bus and is instead riding with Tommy. No one has noticed because our schedules are all mixed up with Abuelo in the hospital. Ileana's absence means that I have to prepare Ana Mari her snack and help her with homework. We usually eat rice pudding Mami has made or cream cheese with guava shells. I also clean whatever room Mami has told me we should clean. The living room was scheduled for today, so I dusted the coffee table and I shook those heavy cushions from the old sofa over and over again until I felt my arms about to fall off. (One of Papi's coworkers at the hospital gave us the sofa. It's in pretty good shape, though it is an ugly green color, like split pea soup.) I also swept and mopped the terrazzo floor.

It's not fair that I'm doing all the work alone, but if I tell Mami, Ileana will get in trouble. Ileana said that if I loved her, I would be a good little sister and keep my mouth shut. When she said this, she pinched her lips together. I don't know what to do, but if she makes me help her with the laundry folding on

Saturday, I'm going to tell. She should have to do *all* the folding.

Saturday, 20th of January

Abuelo returned home again from the hospital, and we went to visit him at Tío Pablo's. He looks awful. Like a skeleton. His eyes are sunken into his cheeks. His skin is the color of chalk, and he has bruises all over his arms. He said the bruises happen when the nurses try to put in the intravenous medicines and supplements. I'm glad I wasn't at the hospital to see all that butchering.

Abuela María was busy all afternoon making lentil soup. She will fatten him up in no time because she is the best cook in the family. When we were in the kitchen and she was chopping up the potatoes and the chunks of ham, she was crying very softly. I hugged her hard. Now I'm a whole head taller than she is. I am growing, that's true, but I also think she is shrinking down while Abuelo is shrinking side-ways. Ana Mari said that our grandparents look like gnomes, these little people in the picture books she likes to read. When we got home, she showed me.

She's right, except Abuela and Abuelo don't have the funny noses or the warts.

Later

I know I shouldn't have gone, but Ileana talked me into it. Together we snuck out and met Tommy at the corner, then we drove several blocks to a party given by a brother and sister whose parents were out of town. It was very noisy, and many of Ileana's friends were drinking beer. She introduced me to a boy who is in the tenth grade. He seemed very nice and was — thank goodness — taller than I was. We talked for a while, but when he found out I went to Citrus Grove Junior High, he couldn't get away from me fast enough. It took me a while after that to find Ileana. She was in the backyard talking. When she spotted me, she leaned over to Tommy and I could tell they started having an argument. On the drive home we didn't talk to each other. Now I'm too wound up to go to sleep.

Sunday, 21st of January

Ana Mari has taught Ileana and me a new American song in English. It goes like this: "This land is your land, this land is my land / From California to the New York island, / From the redwood forest, to the Gulf Stream waters, / This land was made for you and me."

We sang it together for Abuelo Tony, and we sounded very good, almost like the Supremes. It made him smile from ear to ear. It also made me remember all those times he and Abuela baby-sat us back in Cuba. With the radio music on, I would stand on his shoes and we would waltz around the living room, round and round until I got dizzy. Sometimes he would go so fast that I would have to hold hard to his belt buckle. He also taught Ileana how to cha-cha and mambo because he said every self-respecting Cuban should know how to dance. It's in our blood, our music, he said. Tonight I will pray just for him. Usually I pray for Pepito because I figure he needs it most, but I think Pepito can wait a night or two. I pray to La Virgencita del Cobre because Mami says that Jesus cannot ever turn down a request from his mother. So, Mother in heaven, please take care of my grandfather.

At mass this morning I almost fell asleep. Ileana kept elbowing me to stay awake. Mami is now worried that I am coming down with a flu. If she only knew! I won't even tell Jane, and you can bet I won't go out again. It is too risky.

Monday, 22nd of January

Mami always says that life is full of surprises and, dear friend, she is absolutely right. The person I least expected to see again came into homeroom this morning during the public announcements. At first I thought it was odd how much the new student looked like the girl I had left behind in the special country school. But as soon as she turned around to walk to the empty seat in front of me, I knew it was her. I immediately shouted her name: "Alina!"

She was so happy to see me. You should have seen the relief on her face, and I know why. I still remember what it was like to not know anybody in school. It is so awful to be a stranger, to not recognize any hallway or classroom or teacher. It is even worse not to understand what others are saying to you. Of course, it is getting a little better now because there are more Cubans in school. A few teachers speak Spanish, too. Still, that sense of not belonging anywhere is terrible.

The other day Tío Pablo said he hears Spanish in a lot more places now, especially where he and Papi work. He also said that every week four thousand people arrive from the island on the Freedom Flights, that airplane ride we took to come to Miami. Some move north, but many stay here. And even those who move somewhere else eventually return to Miami because they do not like the cold weather. Mami's cousin lived in a place called Buffalo for five years and just moved back last month. She hated the snow. I think I would like the snow — at least for a day or two.

Alina and I share the same homeroom and lunch period, but we do not have any classes together. I was still able to show her around. I could tell she was very nervous, but I told her that's exactly how I felt for a long time. Not anymore, though. We talked a little about some of the other girls who were with us in the country school. Neither of us liked any of them too much. She also told me that Ofelia now attends a special school on the outskirts of the capital and that her parents are planning to send Ofelia and her older brother to Russia to study. Poor Ofelia!

Alina says the best thing about leaving Cuba is knowing that nobody will call her Granito anymore! She made me promise I would never bring that up. Alina came here with her brother, who is in the sixth grade, and her mother. Her parents got divorced because her father became a big Communist and wanted her mother to do the same, but she refused. Alina's grandparents live here, too. She loves her grandparents but misses her father. They plan to write each other every week. I didn't dare tell her about Pepito and how we hardly ever hear from him. Why make her suffer more?

Tuesday, 23rd of January

Starting today we are supposed to go to Tío Pablo's house after school so that Abuela María can watch us there. Mami will fetch us when she returns from work. It will be interesting to find out what excuse Ileana will use to explain her tardiness. I tried to tell her she's going to get into trouble by allowing Tommy to bring her home and sneaking out to those parties, but she pinched my arm and told me to mind my own business.

Thursday, 25th of January

My English is improving day by day. I now have a part in a short play we will perform in class. I speak only a few lines, but I feel proud to have been chosen. At lunchtime Alina and Jane help me memorize my part. At home I practice my lines in front of the mirror. Everyone has noticed how my English is getting better, but sometimes I wonder if that means I will forget Spanish. If I know both languages equally, in what language will I think? How will I dream? How will I pray? Already I know the names for certain things in English but not in Spanish. I've learned them in school and have to ask Papi or Mami to translate the word into Spanish.

Friday, 26th of January

When Abuela María asked Ileana why she has been late all this week, Ileana said she is helping with props and painting scenery for a spring play at school. I am sure she is lying. I think Abuela is suspicious, too, because she narrowed her eyes at Ileana and reminded her that the devil knows more for being old than for being a devil. Ileana should be careful.

Every afternoon just before the sun sets, Ana Mari and I take Abuelo Tony for a walk. He's as slow as a snail but he needs to exercise, so we try to be patient. Along the way he tells us the names of the trees, flowers, and bushes we see, so now I know all about the ixoras, royal poincianas, gumbo-limbos, banyans, impatiens, jacarandas, and floss-silk trees. He said that when he was young, he wanted to work with plants, but his parents made him study medicine because his father was a country doctor. He liked medicine, but now that he is old, he wishes he had paid attention to his dreams. He asked if we were interested in a particular subject in school. Neither Ana Mari nor I have any favorites, though I think I am good in mathematics. Follow your heart, he told us, because that will make you happier.

Monday, 29th of January

I did not mess up any of my lines during the performance in English class. Not once. But I did feel my face getting red when I spoke in front of all my classmates. I wish Mami and Papi could have seen me.

Tuesday, 30th of January

Jane showed me a letter from her grandparents. They again invited me on their summer car trip when they tour the state of Florida. I told Papi about it again, but he waved me away. "We'll be back in Havana by summer," he said. I turned to Mami, but she refused to even consider it. I think I will have to work very hard to convince them. But I must! It would be so exciting to visit different cities and see the rest of this state.

Thursday, 1st of February

Something big is going on in the world because Abuelo and Abuela are glued to the radio. They listen to a show in Spanish called *La Voz del Pueblo,* "The Voice of the People." Ileana explained to me that horrible things are happening in the war in Vietnam.

Tommy and some older boys who are in the local university want to plan a march to protest the war. She wants to join Tommy and wave placards just like the college students we see on TV. Ileana is really asking for trouble now.

Saturday, 3rd of February

Trouble found us. More tomorrow.

Sunday, 4th of February

It was bound to happen. Mami caught us sneaking back into the house. She was waiting for us in the living room, smoking a cigarette. I have never ever seen her smoke. She must have been horribly nervous. As soon as we walked in, she flicked on the lights and stubbed the cigarette in an ashtray. I thought I was going to faint when I saw her face. She yanked me by the hair into her bedroom and went back to the living room to scream at Ileana. The racket woke up Ana Mari, who, as usual, began to cry. When Mami had finished hollering, she made us sit in the kitchen and tell her where we were and what we had done. Ileana went first, and she swore that she was the one responsible for taking me. She insisted I not be punished. That was nice of her. Truth is, I went because I wanted to, even though I had been reminding myself these past days that going to those parties would only bring us grief. Part of me knew the danger, but another part of me liked the attention from the boys — as long as I didn't tell them I was in eighth grade! Mami told Ileana she should be ashamed of herself for leading me down the wrong path, and she made us promise we would not try anything like this again. She said she won't tell Papi. "If he finds out, it would be like a knife through his heart," she explained. Thank goodness he was away for the weekend on one of his training missions. Dealing with him would have been twice as difficult.

She still punished us. I cannot talk on the phone for a week. Neither can Ileana, and she must also stop seeing Tommy on the sly. I hope this will not ruin my chances to take the car trip with Jane and her grandparents. Now I don't dare bring it up until Mami calms down.

"You come from a good family," she told my sister. "You are not a tramp or a nobody. You cannot meet men anywhere they want to and at any time. If a young man wants to court you, he must do so the correct way."

She then lectured us about a girl's virtue being the most important quality she can give her husband. *Los americanos*, she said, give virtue away as if it were no big deal.

Monday, 5th of February

We received two letters from Pepito today. One was dated in August, a few days after we had left, and it was older than the one we got before Christmas. I don't understand why this one took so long to get to us. The second letter was dated in December. They were both short, and his handwriting was very difficult to make out. In the first letter, he writes about how he is building strong muscles because he is getting lots of physical exercise. He has also made new friends and is playing second base and batting third in the lineup. (We don't know what baseball team this could be, but Papi figures it might be from Pepito's own platoon.) He asks Ileana to save him any magazine stories about Elvis Presley and the Beatles. He sounds just like Pepito. But in the second letter, a whole section is blacked out in pen. Papi said that is what the Cuban government censors do if a letter writer reveals something that makes the government look bad. I wonder what that could be. Maybe something awful has happened to Pepito. Maybe they are feeding him food with worms and making him do horrible things. The other parts of the letter we can read fine, but he doesn't sound as upbeat as in the one from August. He writes that he misses us and is sorry that he will not see us for a long time. "I fear that Ana Mari will forget what my face looks like." That's what he wrote. "I will not forget her or her laughter. Does she still laugh like a hyena?" (Ana Mari did not like this part of the letter, but what Pepito writes is true. She does have a funny laugh.)

As I listened to the letter being read aloud, I felt my eyes grow hot. I looked over at Mami, but she was not crying. She was staring straight ahead with a hard face, her chin jutting out. The rest of the night she was very absentminded. She even burned the chicken in the oven, and we had to pull the toasty skin off and eat the rest because we can't afford to throw food away. The chicken was hard and rubbery.

Tuesday, 6th of February

A group of teenage boys threw eggs at Alina's first-floor apartment. They scared her grandparents, mother, and little brother half to death. "Go back where you came from!" they shouted. And they also screamed, "Spics!"

Alina has no idea who these boys might be. She is certain they do not live in her apartment building. The incident upset her mother tremendously. She and her grandmother had to clean the egg goo that came through the window screen, and it stained the sofa.

Alina's mother now makes sure the windows are closed at all times, which turns the inside of the apartment into a furnace. The family must go around in their underwear and sit in front of the fans to keep cool. Alina says it is impossible to concentrate on homework. She dreams of moving to New York or to Chicago because she has read that it snows there a lot and that no one is ever hot. I feel sorry for Alina, but I do not know what to do.

Mami still works at the shoe factory and Tía Carmen at that laundry place, but now they have new night jobs. Abuela helps them. They are sewing pearls and sequins on sweaters and are paid by the piece. A man delivers the sweaters in one big box, and the sequins and pearls in another. He is a friend of Efraín's boss at the craft store, and he allows them to work from home, which is why they took the job. At first Papi didn't want Mami to do it because it would mean more time away from us girls, but she assured him that she would work only after dinner and after we had finished our homework.

Mami and Papi fight often. We can hear them from our bedroom sometimes. They fight about the usual things — Mami working, Papi training with the military, Mami spending too much money, Papi not planning ahead. Maybe it is normal for husbands and wives to fight. I sure hope it doesn't mean anything more than that, though. A divorce always makes the children miss one of the parents. Look what has happened to Alina and Jane.

Thursday, 8th of February

I really miss using the phone. At the end of the school day I have so much to tell Jane that I feel I'm bursting with news. But then I've got to hold it all night until I see her in homeroom the next morning. I should have known we would eventually get caught.

Ileana has been very quiet this week. I wonder if she has talked to Tommy about our punishment.

Two more days until I can use the phone again.

Saturday, 10th of February

Papi got hurt during one of his military training exercises. It wasn't serious, but he came home early this weekend, with a swollen ankle. Tío Pablo told him he had to stay off his feet as much as possible for the next few days. Mami is furious.

I'm glad he came home, though. This afternoon, he and I ate this brown spread — *los americanos* call it peanut butter — on soda crackers from the Cuban bakery and laughed about the way it stuck to the roofs of our mouths. "Silly, silly girl," he called me, and gave me a big hug.

Today when we were helping Abuelo Tony exercise, he asked Ana Mari and me what we remembered about Cuba. I told him about my school and the tile on the kitchen counter and the narrow cobblestone streets in Old Havana and the white sand on the beach of Santa María del Mar and the buttery taste of the Panque Jamaica cupcakes, and the two cane-back rocking chairs on our porch and the wrought-iron front gate that creaked and my pink chenille bedspread and the tall, tall palms on the winding road to my uncle's farm and the *guarapo* juice we would drink in the little bodega the next block over. Actually, we remembered a lot.

"I hope you will always remember your homeland in that way," he told us. His voice sounded funny, like he was about to cry. Then Ana Mari reminded Abuelo that Papi said we might be back home by summer because the people in the island no longer want a bad government and they are tired of not having enough to eat and having to wait in line for everything, including toilet paper. So Abuelo opened his mouth to say something, but he seemed to change his mind. He just motioned for us to keep walking. Later we stopped by a tree with yellow flowers and he asked us its name. "Christmas candle tree," I shouted immediately. Abuelo clapped his hands. Then he told us the name in Latin, but I have already forgotten.

I have been thinking about what Abuelo said about never forgetting your homeland. Sometimes I worry that I will, because I close my eyes and there are faces and places, even decorations in our house, that I cannot remember in detail. It makes me worry about whether or not I have a home. And I mean *home,* not *house.* I have a house in Cuba, in my neighborhood of La Víbora, but I also have a house here. Which one is really home?

I asked Ileana this after dinner tonight, and she looked at me as if I had just landed in a spaceship. Then she sat close to me on the old pea-green sofa and hugged me. I don't know whatever for, because she hasn't done that in a long, long time. She didn't say anything, just patted me on the back. But finally she spoke, and the more I think about her words, the more I realize she is right. She told me that home is where the heart is. It is where your loved ones are and where you feel comfortable hanging around in your pajamas with curlers in your hair. Well then, that means I have a home here and a home across the ocean there, always there.

Monday, 19th of February

I did not forget you. I was just too busy to write. Between homework, cleaning the house, and helping Abuelo to exercise, all my time seems taken up. Then to add to all this, Mami and Tía Carmen got a new order for embroidered sweaters. The man from the factory was so happy with their work that he brought over double the amount from the first time. This means that Mami and Tía Carmen have asked us to help by organizing the sequins and pearls in a special way that makes it easier to sew them on the sweaters. Ileana and I also help pin the design patterns on the front. Ileana said that if she can do this for free, then she should get a job for money at the Grand Union as a checkout girl. Mami said she was much too young, though now she is seventeen, the same age Efraín was when he began working at the Tandy craft store. Boys are different, Tía Carmen and Mami said at the same time. Not in this country, Ileana told them right back.

Tuesday, 20th of February

Papi got a raise. He was moved to the purchasing department in the hospital, too, where he has more work. For dinner he took us to a hamburger place on Northwest Seventh Street called Burger Castle. It has a giant lighted statue of a man with a crown on his head. We ate hamburgers, french fries, and milkshakes. What a splurge!

Wednesday, 21st of February

Efraín has found a job for Ileana at the craft store where he works. Now she wants me to help convince Mami and Papi to allow her to do this. I think this is a wonderful opportunity because if Efraín can work, so should Ileana. But my parents will never listen to that reasoning. I am sure they will come up with some excuse. Why do I know this? Because when I talked to Mami about the car trip this summer, she told me she would have to discuss it with Papi. Well I know what he is going to say.

Friday, 23rd of February

I hate to say this, but I was right. Papi refused to allow Ileana to work with Efraín. He said she was much too young and inexperienced, especially if she planned to work in a city full of wolves. That's just how he said it. What wolves? She would be working with Efraín and his boss and the boss's wife. We have already met them, and they are very nice. They have been good to Efraín, too. I can only imagine what Papi will tell me when I bring up the subject of Jane's grandparents' trip again.

Ileana argued that she would always be inexperienced if she remained imprisoned in her own home. Mami defended her, which surprised me, but Papi would not budge. He can be so mean sometimes. Whoever made him the boss? I wish Mami would stand up to him more. She is always skulking around so as not to upset him. I wonder what he will say when he finds out that Mami has learned to drive with Efraín and Tía Carmen. He better not cause a scene. Instead, he better be proud of her. Mami is trying so hard to be brave and to adapt to this new life.

Papi bought a car! It was a big surprise. He didn't say a word to anybody when he and Mami left this morning to run errands. We thought they were going to visit somebody in the hospital because we were not allowed to go along, but the last thing I ever thought could happen was this. Our very own automobile!

It is a 1954 Plymouth station wagon, and Papi bought it from the father of a man who works with him. It is green, and the inside is in good shape for being an old car. The three of us girls fit comfortably in the back. Papi drove us around the block and over to Tío Pablo's, and then everybody took turns going for a ride, even Abuela María, who whooped and hollered like a little girl. After Tía Carmen made *café,* Mami told Papi she had something to show him. He gave her a funny look, and we all went outside to watch as Mami got into the driver's side and took Papi on his own ride. When they returned, he was pale. Papi told Tía Carmen that she had done a good job teaching Mami to drive but that Mami needed more practice making turns. Scared him half to death when she took a right turn going too fast, he said. Tío Pablo and Abuelo Tony punched Papi in the arm and slapped him on the back. I was surprised but also relieved that he was not angry.

Now that we have a car, I suppose it means that we are not going back to Cuba anytime soon.

Tuesday, 27th of February

There is a new boy in class. He is so cute! Jane nearly faints every time he walks by her. He is Cuban, but he is from somewhere up north. He is in almost all my classes, but I do not dare talk to him. I wouldn't know what to say. Besides, I worry about how I look. One day my face appears normal, like it belongs to me. Other days, I look in the mirror and my nose is too big and my mouth looks crooked and one eye is smaller than the other. I also wish my hair weren't so straight. It droops down over my ears like short wet noodles. Maybe I need another haircut. Or maybe I should grow it out again. Good thing I do not have any pimples. Poor Alina!

Wednesday, 28th of February

When Ileana gets something in her head, she won't let it go. Today again she asked if she could work with Efraín. And again Papi said no. Can I expect any different with my request for the car trip?

I finally asked her about Tommy, and she shrugged her shoulders. "Who would want a girlfriend who can't go anywhere?" she asked me. "I might as well be in jail." If Tommy isn't her boyfriend anymore, she probably won't participate in any protest marches against the war. Thank goodness! Papi would be very upset if she did something like that.

Thursday, 29th of February

This is unbelievable! Absolutely unbelievable! When I was walking with Abuelo Tony, we ran into that new boy from school. His name is Juan Carlos, and he lives two blocks from my uncle's house. Jane is right. He is very cute, but I am taller than he is. And his voice is kind of squeaky. We talked to him for a few minutes. Actually, Abuelo talked to him, and he was very polite. I was too embarrassed and stared at the cracks in the sidewalk.

Friday, 1st of March

We did not see Juan Carlos on our afternoon walk, but Abuelo showed us the parts of a flower from an ixora bush. I already knew their names in Spanish and now, because of Abuelo, I know them in Latin. I suppose soon I will learn them in English, too. Three languages — imagine.

Saturday, 2nd of March

We went to the most fantastic store today. It is called La Tijera and it's on Flagler Street and Twelfth Avenue. Mami and Tía Carmen came here to buy things for the house when we first moved. Everything is made just the way they were in Cuba. We saw Cuban-style mops, wash pans, coffee cups, and aluminum drinking cups to boil milk. I almost felt like I was back on the island. Truth is, of course, no store back on the island would have had so many goods on the shelves. Besides, people would not have been able to buy anything unless they had the correct ration coupon.

Though we looked at a lot of things, we bought only what we needed. Tía Carmen got herself a meat grinder just like the one she had in Cuba. Mami needed a washboard and a wooden mortar and pestle to smash garlic. She also bought an aluminum mold for flan and a wood plantain-chip maker. I hope Papi doesn't complain that these necessities were a waste of money. Those are usually the first words out of his mouth when we show him any purchase — even toilet paper!

Before we left, Tía Carmen pointed to the men, three brothers, who own the store. They opened it when they realized people like my parents needed household stuff but preferred to buy what they recognized. She said that if you drive around Flagler or Southwest Eighth Street, there are lots of little shops opened by Cubans in the past three or four years. There is a Chinese Cuban restaurant, a religious goods store, several bakeries, and even a botanica that sells supplies for priests of Santeria. I wonder if Papi has seen these shops. If so, what must he think? I know what I think: Those people won't be returning to Cuba anytime soon.

Sunday, 3rd of March

I played dominoes with the grown-ups today and won. I was Papi's partner because Mami was in the kitchen scrubbing the dirty pans from our big Sunday lunch. Usually Tío Pablo and Tía Carmen win because they are very good domino players, and they are also lucky. Efraín and Ileana sometimes play, but they don't pay much attention to the game. Actually, Efraín usually partners with Abuelo Tony, but Abuelo was too tired and took a nap instead. So Efraín convinced Ileana to stop looking through her fashion magazines and be a good cousin — which meant he wanted her as partner. Good cousin or not, the two of them played horribly together. Ileana didn't pay much attention to the game, so she didn't keep track of which player lacked which number. To me, that is the whole challenge of the game.

When we lived in Cuba, my family used to play dominoes every winter Sunday after mass and lunch. Both sets of grandparents and uncles participated. Cousins, too. The matches took hours, especially if only the men played and smoked their cigars and sipped their *café*. Abuela always used to make a flan, and Tía Carmen's specialty was *torejas*.

Thinking about all this makes me very hungry. My mouth is watering for the syrup of the *torejas*. I realize I have not eaten any since we arrived in Miami.

Monday, 4th of March

Remember the two men in gray suits who took Papi to their office for questioning several months ago? They showed up on our doorstep again tonight, this time with a third man who speaks Spanish. In the middle of us doing homework and Mami and Tía Carmen sewing the sequins on the sweaters, no less.

They were very polite, though. They talked to Papi for almost two hours in the kitchen. Mami could hardly keep her hands steady to thread a needle. After they left, everyone pretended as if nothing had happened. Everyone but Mami, who threw the sweater into her sewing basket and marched out of the room. Papi followed her. When they both returned to the living room, I could tell they had had a fight because Mami's lips were set tight and a vein on Papi's forehead pulsed.

Wednesday, 6th of March

I received another perfect mark on my mathematics test. And Ana Mari was the third-best speller in the spelling bee in her class. She got a yellow ribbon, and Mami showed it off to the whole family.

Thursday, 7th of March

Tonight at dinner Papi surprised us all by announcing that after much thought he has decided to allow Ileana to work with Efraín at the craft store — *as long as it does not interfere with her studies.* He said that last part as if it were in capital letters. I think Mami knew something about this beforehand, but Ileana and the rest of us were caught off guard. You should have seen Ileana's face. Eyes wide then narrowing with suspicion, she looked like the black beans and rice inside her mouth had turned too hot. As soon as dinner was over, she phoned Efraín. They agreed she would meet him at the craft store after school tomorrow.

Saturday, 9th of March

Ileana began work today. She came home wearing a white apron and her hair tied back in a bun. She looked very grown-up. She let me watch all the shows I wanted on the television and did not complain to Mami once.

Also today, Mami took her driver's license test and is now allowed to drive the car. She is so proud of herself that she beams like a lighthouse. She is trying to practice as much as she can, driving herself to the Grand Union or to the pharmacy — anywhere to do an errand. She always invites us to come along, but truth is, sometimes I get nervous when she drives. She concentrates so hard on the road and the steering wheel that her face is all scrunched up. She doesn't let us put the radio on, either, or even talk among ourselves. Not at all like Papi, who sometimes drives with his right hand while his left arm hangs out the open window. He has a funny tan line from that.

Finally, another important event: Tío Pablo took the last of his licensing examinations to become a doctor in this country. He won't know the results right away, but he thinks he did well. I hope so. He has studied a lot.

Tuesday, 12th of March

I am trying to help Alina as much as I can with her homework, and she is improving tremendously in math. Her English is also getting better, but since she does not like to read, her vocabulary is limited. At Jane's suggestion, I passed on the Nancy Drew books. Maybe she will be interested in those.

Wednesday, 13th of March

Ileana loves her job. Every night she tells us a story about a customer or about Mr. F. Everybody calls the owner by the first initial of his last name because his name is very long, and we don't know how to pronounce it. Today a woman in a very fancy suit came to the store, and she bought three dozen purse kits with a seashell pattern. She asked them to be shipped to her home in New York. Then she gave both Efraín and Ileana a dollar tip!

Friday, 15th of March

I did not walk with Abuelo Tony today because after school Mami asked me to accompany her and Tía

Carmen to a shop where packages of medicine are bundled and sent to Cuba. Our package contained aspirins, vitamins, cotton balls, two pairs of glasses, Mercurochrome, gauze, adhesive strips, a medicine for diarrhea, and a few other vials with names I did not recognize. When I asked Mami how much all that costs to mail, she said, "An eye in your head." Later, though, she told me that the package was worth every penny because my grandparents cannot find any of those medicines in Cuba. As we were leaving, more and more people were lining up in the store to send their relatives what they need. Tía Carmen said that on Saturdays you cannot even get in the door because it is so busy.

Jane is preparing to have a slumber party for her birthday next month. Mrs. Henderson said Jane can invite five girls for pizza and a sleep-over. I have never been to a slumber party. That is very much an American concept. All my birthday parties in Cuba were at my house on a Sunday afternoon. We ate *croquetas, bocaditos,* and *pastelitos,* and all the family came, even my great-aunts and great-uncles. We played pin-the-tail-on-the-donkey with our cousins and broke a big piñata in the backyard. Remembering those parties makes me both happy and sad — happy because I had so much fun and sad because I know all the cousins will not be together again for some time.

I have already told Mami about this slumber party and that it involves me sleeping at Jane's house. I explained to her that I would sleep in a sleeping bag borrowed from Mrs. Henderson and that after pizza and punch, all the girls brush and curl each other's hair and paint their nails. (I am not allowed to do that, or pluck my eyebrows, until I am fifteen.) Jane said we will also listen to the radio or the record player, and then dance to the music all we want. Mami had never heard of this type of party and promised to consult with Papi. Well, I know exactly what he is going to say. Why can't she make the decision herself? I think I am going to ask Jane's mother to call and talk to Mami.

I figure that if I am allowed to attend this party and everything turns out right, I can work myself up to the summer car trip. I know I've already planted the seed in both Mami's and Papi's heads. Now I have to wait for it to take root, then let it blossom. I think that's the type of advice Abuelo would give me. I can only hope

Mami has forgotten about us sneaking out in the middle of the night.

Saturday, 16th of March

Something horrible has happened, but I am not sure what it is. A couple of hours ago, Tío Pablo rushed into the house wanting to know where Papi was. He was frantic. He told Mami to turn on the radio as soon as he walked in the door. A long time passed before we heard a news bulletin that reported several Cuban men had been arrested while leaving Key West in a boat full of weapons heading for Cuba. Tío Pablo wanted to know if Papi had mentioned anything about leaving the country. Mami shook her head and kept wringing her hands until Tío Pablo had her sit down on the living room couch. He told me to serve Mami ice water and stay with her until the rest of the family came to keep us company. He made a few phone calls, and now we are waiting for more news.

I am trying not to think too much about the news reports, but it is difficult for me to concentrate on anything else. My mind wanders right back to what the radio announcer said. Can my father be one of the seven men taken to prison in Key West? I cannot imagine Papi dressed up as a soldier and getting on a boat to go to Cuba with guns and bombs. And at night, too. That is very dangerous. I like to think of his military training weekends as something he does for practice but not for real.

Virgencita, Mother of God, I know that I do not always faithfully recite my prayers. I sometimes forget before going to sleep, but please take care of Papi.

Later

Everyone is here watching television, even Abuelo Tony, who doesn't go out much at night because of his health. We have not heard from Papi, but that is not unusual. On the weekends he leaves, he does not phone or return until Sunday afternoon or evening. It is so hard to wait.

If Papi has been arrested, Tío Pablo thinks he will call to let us know. We might also learn who has been arrested if the news announcers recite the men's names. The names may also be in the morning paper, but tomorrow seems such a long, long way off.

Mami is taking this very calmly. Abuela María, though, is very upset. She paces the room and has called her cousin in New Jersey twice. He works for the government in a town up there, and she thinks he may have connections to help us. When she says this aloud, Tío Pablo rolls his eyes.

Before bed

No word yet. The news show at 11 P.M. did not reveal any names, either. I am too tired for words.

Sunday, 17th of March

When I woke this morning, Mami was gone and Abuela María was making coffee in the kitchen. She told me that all the grown-ups had left for Key West very, very early. "Does this mean Papi was arrested?" I demanded. But Abuela just put her hand up to stop my words. She insisted I sit down to breakfast. I ate, though my stomach was all in knots.

Close to midmorning Mami called to say they had found Papi and would be driving back later in the day. Did that mean Papi was returning with them? Where were they calling from? Was he one of the seven men arrested? I was full of questions, but Abuela still wasn't certain about — or wasn't telling me — any answers.

The rest of the day took forever. I finished my homework and played Parcheesi with Ana Mari. Abuelo Tony took us for a walk and tried to cheer us up. "Things happen for a reason," he kept telling us. But what things? I hate not knowing. I also phoned Jane and Alina several times, but was too embarrassed to tell them about Papi at first. I was scared that if their mothers found out my father had been arrested, they would not be allowed to be my friends.

By nighttime, though, I broke down and told them. Both wanted to come over to console me, but Abuela said this was not the right time. Instead we talked on the phone, and they kept telling me not to worry, that everything was going to turn out all right. But now it's time to go to bed — I can hear Abuela yelling for us to turn off the lights — and I still don't know where my parents are or why my father was in Key West. If my head was not pounding so hard and my stomach wasn't rumbling so furiously, I think I would have the energy to pray.

Monday, 18th of March

Papi was home by the time we returned from school. I ran up to him and gave him a big hug. I was so relieved to see him. Then I asked a million questions. He said he was not arrested with the seven men, but he was in a second boat a few yards away with two others, so he was taken in for questioning. He looked like he hadn't slept all night.

Mami didn't look any better, and she was very angry. Just a little while ago, they had a huge argument, the same argument they've had a million times. She wants him to quit the training.

"What if you do go to Cuba?" she asked. "What if you and Pepito are in the same battlefield but on opposite sides?"

Papi didn't answer. All he said was that it was his duty to fight for the liberation of his country and that he could not look in the mirror if he turned his back on those who remained on the island.

I don't know what to think. I can understand how Mami feels. She wants Papi to be home with us, to help her start a new life here. When he goes away on weekends, I sometimes think he is being selfish. But then, when I look at things from Papi's side, I also realize why he does what he does. He loves Cuba very much, and he hates to see the island with a bad government.

Oh, I am so confused!

Tuesday, 19th of March

I found out that Ileana still belongs to that peace group at school. Her school notebook is full of flyers Tommy wants her to hand out before the first school bell rings. She drew up the flyers herself. I warned her to be careful around Mami, but she ignored me. She wasn't mean about it, but she said I was too young to understand that sometimes a person must speak out for what she believes in and not worry about what others are going to say. Ileana feels it is important to take action, not just sit and hope for something to happen. Does this sound familiar? Now I know how Mami feels when Papi ignores her warnings.

Friday, 22nd of March

I got the invitation for Jane's birthday. It is scheduled for two weeks from tomorrow, after Easter break. I showed it to Mami and she promised to bring it up with Papi. I also gave her all my school papers with good marks for the week. I figure it can't hurt to show her what a good student I am.

Thursday, 28th of March

An almost perfect mark in mathematics — a 95. I could have gotten 100 if I had not made a stupid arithmetic mistake. Next time I will check my work more carefully. Of course, I made sure to give this paper to Mami as well.

Sunday, 31st of March

Palm Sunday. We were able to get several dried fronds at church, and Abuela María and Abuelo Tony are teaching me how to weave them together to make special holy decorations for the door. Efraín is especially talented at this. He made a crown for Ana Mari, and she now wants to wear it to her First Communion in May, which made us all laugh because she doesn't understand the frond will dry and become too brittle to do anything except hang by the door to bless a room.

Efraín said he learned to do fancy frond weaving in Cuba from a little monk who used to make all kinds of elaborate weaves and sell them in front of the cathedral. I'm not sure if Efraín is telling the truth. He exaggerates just to see how gullible we are.

Monday, 1st of April

Efraín is such a jokester. He and Ileana rushed home from work today and insisted we turn on the radio immediately. Efraín claimed he had heard a news bulletin about the United States invading Cuba. As you can imagine, that got Papi and Tío Pablo all excited. They not only turned on the radio, but the television set, too. They even phoned their friends and relatives. No one had heard anything, but everyone else also tuned in to the news. Abuela María started to clap, but Mami cried because she was worried that Pepito would have to fight against the American marines. All this discussion and listening for news lasted well over an hour until Efraín shouted, "April fool!" It was all a joke. We didn't even know there was such a day as April Fools'. In Cuba practical jokes are usually played out on December 28.

I thought it was very clever, but none of the grown-ups was amused. Papi said certain subjects should never be joked about, and the liberation of Cuba is one of them. Afterward Efraín felt terrible and he hung his head as if his best friend had died. I tried to console him, but it didn't work.

Later I called Jane and played a trick on her. I made up this story about meeting Juan Carlos again when Abuelo and I took a walk. I said that he had invited me to the movies, which of course is the biggest, fattest lie in the world. He doesn't know either Jane or I exist, and besides, I would never be allowed to go out anywhere by myself, and certainly not with a boy. I had her believing every little detail until I couldn't come up with any more, and that's when I singsonged, "April fool!"

Wednesday, 3rd of April

I finished the book Efraín brought me from the library, and I plan to read two more during Easter break. It makes the time go by faster.

Abuela María is also teaching me to cook. This afternoon I watched her make *picadillo* and helped by chopping up the onions and slicing the green peppers. It is not as easy as it looks, working with the knife, and I do things slowly because I'm scared of slicing off my finger.

To be honest, it's not so much the mixing of ingredients that I like as the bustling about in the warmth of the kitchen and the mouthwatering smell of the seasoning. I also enjoy listening to my grandmother's humming, which remains constant whether she's chopping, stirring, or slicing.

Sunday, 7th of April

You should have seen Saint Michael's today. Mass was packed with people standing along the aisles and all around the back. Everyone was dressed so pretty. All the girls wore white patent leather shoes and matching purses, little straw hats and white gloves. It was such a fashion display that I felt like a country bumpkin. Tía Carmen said that next year, when we have a little more money, she will take us shopping for Easter dresses and hats. But Papi told her that next year we would be taking Communion in Cuba.

Tuesday, the 9th of April

We are living in dark times, that is what Abuelo Tony says, and everybody agrees. First there is the war in Vietnam. A week or so ago, President Johnson announced on television that he was stopping the bombing in North Vietnam, a move my father considers terribly wrong. ("To cave in to the Communists like that," Papi groaned, shaking his head. Actually, if it were up to him, he would prefer *los americanos* transfer their attention from Vietnam to Cuba.) But for all this talk of peace, the fighting continues, and so do the marches of young people who think *los americanos* should not be there. Ileana wanted to join some of her friends in a peace march through Bayfront Park next weekend, but my parents will not even consider it.

I do not know what to think about this war so far away. To me, war is bad — all war. We should not kill people. We should sit down and talk about problems and try to come up with a solution. Mami agrees; so does Ileana. My sister said, "If the old men who send the young men to war had to go themselves, I bet you would see a lot more peace treaties." But Papi says that only force changes people. When he says this, then I change my mind because I think of what is happening in my country. You have to take back what is yours, grab it away, because nobody ever just returns it.

Also today in school we watched the memorial services for Martin Luther King, Jr., the Negro leader who was assassinated last Thursday. It is so sad. Srta. Reed cried during Mr. King's funeral. Her family is from Chicago, and there have been riots there and in other cities because of the assassination. It is scary to see the fires blazing in these neighborhoods, the mothers weeping, and the young people marching with their fists in the air. Due to all this commotion, Mami is afraid for Papi because there have been a few problems between police and residents in the neighborhood near Jackson Memorial Hospital. My father likes to tease her by saying that if he dies in this country, we need to make sure his ashes are sent back home. Mami does not think this is funny.

On the weekends he does not work overtime, Papi continues to train with his friends. Mami warns Papi that if he is charged with a crime, she will not visit him in jail or go to court. Even I don't believe that!

Honestly, though, my father is too old to be waging any kind of war. He is forty-five years of age and losing his hair. Ileana makes fun of the way he parts his hair now, trying to make the side tendrils cover the thinning on top.

Wednesday, 10th of April

I finally screwed up enough courage to ask Papi myself about going to Jane's slumber party. When I explained to him what it was, I could tell Mami had already spoken to him. He pretended to make a serious face, but then he said . . . YES!

I think — oh, how I hope! — I may have a good chance at traveling with Jane this summer.

Sunday, 14th of April

We had so much fun at the slumber party. I gave Jane a diary as a birthday present. It is a little bigger than this one, and the cover is made of cloth with a bright orange-and-yellow paisley print.

During the party we ate pizza and ice cream, and

Jane painted my nails a bright red. Another girl from school, Sophie, cut my bangs. We hardly slept the whole night. I like this American custom.

Back home, Mami harrumphed when she saw my bangs — they *are* a bit crooked — and she made me remove the nail polish. I am not old enough for that, she says. Well, it was fun while it lasted.

Wednesday, 17th of April

Remember how Papi always tells stories about Cuba during dinner because he is afraid we will forget our homeland? Well, now he has come up with the idea of playing a game. He asks questions about Cuban geography, history, and landmarks, and the person who answers the most correctly gets a reward at the end of the meal. Yesterday it was a guava pastry. Today it was an entire meringue.

Of course Ileana has won both times, which I consider unfair. She is older and has studied more. Then she won't even share any of the desserts because she says she deserves every bite. Tonight Ana Mari cried because she did not get one single question right. Mami told Papi that he needs to be more realistic about our knowledge, especially Ana Mari, who only had one year of schooling in Cuba.

I must admit that even when I lose I still enjoy myself. I like how excited Papi gets when we are playing the game. His eyes shine, and he twirls the tips of his black mustache. Sometimes he even jumps from the table, forcing Mami to say, "Please, José Calixto, we are at the dinner table." But you can tell she doesn't really mean it. It's almost like old times.

Friday, 19th of April

We received a letter from Pepito. He says that sometime in May or June he will be spending a weekend with my grandparents in Havana. This really lifted Mami's spirits because she is hoping we can talk to him by telephone for the first time in almost a year.

Pepito also wrote that he has grown two inches since we last saw him and hopes to send us a photograph soon. It will be very interesting to see how he has changed. He asked after us girls, too, and wrote that he plans to attend the University of Havana to study engineering. This came as a big surprise to all of us because he always talked about being a pilot.

Sunday, 21st of April

In Havana there is a road that winds all through the city along the seawall. It's called El Malecón, and sometimes when you sit on the wall, you get sprayed by the ocean. It is the best feeling in the world. A lot of couples go there just to watch the blue sea stretch out until you can't see it anymore. It's a very romantic spot, especially at night, and I know that Alina's father proposed to her mother there under a full moon. We used to go almost every winter Saturday to sit, and Papi would make up stories about the ships and boats we saw out on the horizon.

Miami does not have a Malecón, Tío Pablo said, so instead we went to El Parque de las Palomas. The Cubans call it Pigeon Park because of all the pigeons, but its real name is Bayfront Park. We brought old bread in a paper bag, and it seemed the pigeons knew this because they quickly flocked to us. Amazing how tame they are, coming right up to our hands. There was one pigeon that looked sick. It was puffed up, and its eyes had yucky stuff oozing from them. The other pigeons were very cruel to it and would flap their wings in the sick one's face and steal crumbs from it. Efraín said that's just how animals are. The stronger ones get the best food, best mates, and best shelter. The group cannot be slowed down by a weak or sick member. Well, I thought that was just plain mean, and I made it a point to feed the sick pigeon. It was afraid to come close to me like the others, so I had to drop crumbs and then wave the stronger birds away.

After we fed the pigeons, we walked around the park's flower gardens and looked across Biscayne Bay through coin telescopes. We saw one fancy yacht, a big one, with several women sitting on deck in very skimpy bathing suits. Efraín whistled at them, but Abuela María gasped and shook her head. She said it was an act of immorality for women to go to the beach almost naked. Then she looked our way and wagged her finger at us in warning. Abuela has nothing to worry about. Can you imagine Papi ever allowing us out of the house in nothing but a bra and panties? Never!

Wednesday, 24th of April

Alina has been absent from school three days. I called her several times this afternoon, but no one answered. I am worried.

Friday, 26th of April

Still no Alina. I asked our homeroom teacher if she knew why Alina was out, but she said the office had not received a call to excuse her absences. Jane said maybe she moved, but that can't be right. She would have told us.

Saturday, 27th of April

I asked Mami to drive by Alina's apartment building. We knocked on her apartment door several times, but nobody answered. All the lights were off, too. I have a bad feeling about this.

I won my first game of Cuban trivia tonight. The question no one knew, but I did — or at least I was the fastest in answering — was: Where and when did Independence hero José Martí die? (Dos Rios, May 1895.) Papi took me to Dairy Queen, and I ordered a vanilla cone dipped in hard chocolate. Hooray for me!

Monday, 29th of April

Alina was in school today. She looked awful, like she had been left in one of those big dryers at the

Laundromat too long. She said her mother is in the hospital for a nervous breakdown. I asked her if that meant the loony bin, and she burst out crying. I felt horrible I had said that. She calmed down after she went to the bathroom and washed her face, but all during homeroom I could hear sniffling. Then at lunch, she wouldn't talk about it. I don't even know if she and her brother are still living with the grandparents. What will happen to them? Will they be sent back to Cuba? Will their father come to take care of them?

I told Mami about Alina, and she said that the best thing I can do is to give her an ear to listen and a shoulder to cry on. Maybe then she will tell me how we can help her. Poor Alina! Just when she was getting used to all the changes in the new country, this happens. I will say a prayer for her tonight.

Tuesday, 30th of April

Alina looked a little better today. She said her grandparents are very old, but they take good care of her. Her grandfather works rolling cigars at a little shop on Southwest Eighth Street. Her grandmother takes care of two children after school, but they do not have enough money to pay all the bills. Alina wants to get a job to help out. She knows of a little cafeteria near school owned by a friend of her grandfather's. The owner is willing to pay her to wash dishes and clean counters and help his wife do whatever is needed. I think Alina is too young. I know Papi would never allow me to work, and Jane says the government in this country does not allow workers our age. We would be considered child labor.

No matter how much we argued, though, Alina didn't budge. She seems intent on working at that cafeteria no matter what and insists she has no choice. Her mother is sick, her grandparents are too old, and her brother is too young. She is the only one strong enough to do something about the family's situation. Besides, she says, the job will be easy compared to laboring in the fields in Cuba. The cafeteria even has air-conditioning.

Wednesday, 1st of May

Today I brought home another perfect exam in mathematics, so I decided I should ask my parents — again but more forcefully — about going on the car trip with Jane and her grandparents. But I hadn't even got the last word out, when Papi said, "I already told you. No! Absolutely not!"

Thursday, 2nd of May

Papi has had a car accident. We are now in a waiting room at his hospital, Jackson Memorial, hoping to hear news. Good news please, dear Virgencita de la Caridad, good news. Mami and Abuela María are with him in the emergency room. A few minutes ago Tío Pablo came to tell us that Papi is scheduled for X rays. He is all right, Tío Pablo insisted, but hurting all over. After the X rays Papi has to undergo other tests. I don't know if all those tests are good or bad, but it must mean that the accident was not just a fender bender. It must be something serious.

I have a very bad headache from holding in the tears.

Later

We are home now, but with no news about Papi. Mami sent us back because it was getting too late. I cannot possibly go to sleep. I keep hearing noises through the windows, and it is so hot, even with the fan on full blast. I wish we had air-conditioning in the bedrooms like Jane has.

Ileana is screaming at me to turn off the lights. I thought she believed in love and peace and all that stuff. What a hypocrite!

In the middle of the night

I still cannot sleep. I am so worried about Papi. Virgencita del Cobre, please watch over my dear Papi. He is a good man, and he takes good care of us, and he always tries to do the right thing. He needs you now, Virgencita.

If only the phone would ring with news. Any news. The silence is what makes me so nervous. It is not really silence if you listen closely, because the house creaks and groans, and the refrigerator hums. But if you forget about those noises, there is a quietness that vibrates. Only the swoosh of my pen can be heard.

Friday, 3rd of May

It is almost 8 A.M., and I must hurry before I run out to the bus stop. Papi has a broken left arm and cuts on his face from the broken windshield. He must stay in the hospital until tomorrow because doctors are watching a bump on his head. It must be a big bump for them to be so careful about it.

Mami already left for the hospital with Tío Pablo, but she woke us up early to let us know that we should not worry about Papi. I couldn't help it, but I burst into tears when she delivered the news. Mami immediately came over and hugged me.

Later Abuela María told us how the accident happened. The other car did not halt at a STOP sign and it hit Papi's car on the driver's side as it was going through the intersection. The other driver is only nineteen years old, and he was going too fast and got hurt very badly.

Sunday, 5th of May

We expected Papi to be home from the hospital, but now he has an infection. I'm not sure what it is, but doctors have to give him antibiotics. If he is not home by Tuesday, Mami promised she would sneak us into his room.

Tuesday, 7th of May

Papi is home! He looks like he's been in a boxing match. He has two black eyes, and his nose is red and crooked. He said his face hit the steering wheel so hard he can't believe he didn't lose any teeth. His left arm is in a cast, and the heat makes the cast itch. We all got to sign our names on it. I wrote, "I love you, Papi," and drew a big heart.

Ileana's boss sent Papi a basket of fruit with a card that said, "Get Well Soon, Mr. and Mrs. F." We thought it was funny that Mr. F. didn't sign his full name, but Papi was very flattered that someone he doesn't know would be so thoughtful. Ileana must be a good worker if the bosses send her father a get-well gift.

Though the accident was horrible, some good has come from it. Mami and Papi are getting along better, and she has convinced him that he should not return to the weekend militia training. I don't know how long that will last, but for now it makes her happy.

Since everybody was in such a good mood, I

brought up the car trip again. As expected, both my parents immediately said no. But — and this is a good, favorable *but* — they listened to me while I explained why I should be allowed to go.

Wednesday, 8th of May

Alina loves her job. She says she feels very grown-up and is learning to cook, too. She is allowed to eat whatever she wants as long as the customers don't see her. She goes every day after school and stays past dinnertime, when the cafeteria closes up. She worked last Saturday morning and hopes to do so again this weekend. I don't know when she will have time to do homework. We have to turn in a project on the American Revolutionary War by the end of the week, and she hasn't even started. I asked her if her mother was getting better, and she shrugged. I was too embarrassed to ask more.

When we were exercise-walking with Abuelo this afternoon, I told him about Alina. He said that many children her age must work to help their parents make ends meet. This does not happen often in the United States, but it does in other countries. We should appreciate the opportunity to live here, he said, and never embarrass our people by doing something foolish. I asked him if he missed Cuba, and he smiled and nodded. Then tears began to roll down his cheeks. One hung on to his chin forever, until he finally wiped it away.

"My dear hearts," he told us, "I think I will die before I see my homeland again."

That is the saddest statement I have ever heard anybody say, and I wish I had tried to convince my grandfather otherwise. But I didn't say anything. I just stood there, frozen, with my eyes wide and my mouth open, staring at Abuelo's tears, then at Ana Mari. She didn't know what to say, either.

Saturday, 11th of May

Ana Mari had the final fitting for her First Communion dress. She looks like an angel in white, with the ruffled skirt and the puff sleeves. My mother has also made her a lovely veil. Abuela María bought her white gloves, and Tía Carmen gave her the most beautiful rosary. The beads are made of glass, and when you hold it up to the light, you can see all kinds of rainbows reflected.

Sunday, 12th of May

For Mother's Day, we each wore a red carnation on our dress in honor of our mother. That's an old Cuban custom. If your mother is dead, as is Abuela María's and Tía Carmen's, you wear a white carnation. Red flowers are for mothers who are alive. We gave Mami a perfume Papi picked out. It is a very expensive perfume she used to wear at home, so the bottle was no bigger than my thumb. The perfume is called Chanel, and it was very popular in Cuba. When she dabbed it on, though, she began to cry. I thought she was upset we had spent so much money on the gift, but later I found out that's not why she was crying. She was sad because Pepito could not be with us to celebrate the day.

"We are not complete when we are living apart," she sobbed.

There is something I have noticed about my family. Or maybe it's not just my family, but all families living in exile. It seems we can never be completely happy. Even when something good happens, something that we can laugh at or celebrate, there is still a sadness buried under our skin, flowing through our veins, because we are not living where we want to be and because we are separated from those we love.

Thursday, 16th of May

The teachers have assigned so much homework this week that I have not had a moment to myself — or for you. But I could not go to bed without writing the good news: My parents have agreed to talk to Jane's grandparents about the trip. They made it clear that this does not mean I will be allowed to go, but it is still a good sign. I don't want to get my hopes up, though. I know that for them to even consider talking about it is a big victory for me. I've also talked to my grandparents and to Tía Carmen about the trip, telling them how much I would learn by going to see such historic sites as Cape Canaveral and Saint Augustine. Having the rest of the family on my side can only help.

More good news: Alina's mother is home, and

Alina is very happy. She refuses to stop working, though, because she says her family needs the money. I also found out that she lied to the couple that owns the cafeteria. She told them she was sixteen, and she is only fourteen.

Ana Mari's First Communion mass was beautiful, and she knew exactly when to bow her head and when to genuflect and when to stick out her tongue for the Host. She is amazing, Mami said, because no one had any time to practice with her or to check to make sure she knew what she was doing. She also knows her prayers in both languages. I can only recite them in Spanish. (She did not wear the Palm Sunday frond crown on her head as she originally said she would. Thank goodness. She did wear the beautiful gloves and held the glass-bead rosary.)

Papi took lots of photographs with Abuelo's camera, including one of the entire family around a table full of *bocaditos*, guava and meat pastries, and a two-tier cake Tía Carmen baked. Papi wants to make several copies of that photograph and send it to Cuba so our relatives can see how abundant food is in this country. I think that would just make them feel horrible about their situation, but I guess Papi wants to show off our good fortune. Let's just hope that Papi's bruises from the car accident don't show up. They are now turning yellow, and he looks like he has a terrible, contagious illness.

Sunday, 19th of May

Just when I thought life was going smoothly, Papi decided to sneak out of the house to go to a luncheon meeting with his militia friends. Mami was so angry! She stomped around the house all afternoon. I am not surprised, though. I think Papi cares too much about returning to Cuba to give up. He will always try to do everything to change the Communist government, and in his mind that means fighting our way back.

Monday, 20th of May

Happy birthday to me! This is my first year celebrating Cuban Independence Day in another country. Papi said we should all be in mourning because our island is not truly free. "We need a new proclamation of independence," he told us at dinner.

Ileana seems to be doing her own proclaiming already. When she offers her opinion on something, Papi says she is waging her own war of independence. I used to wonder about this, but in the last few days I have realized he may be right. Ileana — all of us children — are like a colony, subjected to another bigger, stronger power. Rules are imposed on us, and we have little say in our own affairs. Why can't we have our own opinions on the Vietnam War? Why must my mother decide what I should wear? Why do we have to do everything an adult tells us?

I told this to Mami, who nodded as if she understood, but she really did not. Instead she changed the subject and asked me if I liked my cake. She baked me one for my birthday and filled it with guava jelly. It was so delicious I had three — yes, three! — pieces. Ileana refused to have any because she is on a diet. ("Do you want to look like an *americana,* a walking skeleton?" Abuela María asked her. Abuela María thinks North American women are much too thin.) I will take a piece to school for Jane and Alina. Mrs. Henderson has promised to take us to a movie for my birthday since I did not have a party. When Papi gave his approval to this excursion and even said that it sounded like fun, I was very surprised. Maybe this means he will say yes to the car trip, too. (Ileana, being her usual sarcastic self, said he got some sense knocked into him in the car accident.)

Though it is a year away, Mami is already talking about my *quinces* party. My introduction to society will not be a big affair, but Tía Carmen says one of the customers at the Laundromat where she works is the forelady in a garment factory and perhaps she will be able to find some discounted fabric for my dress. Mami has also begun to look through the bargain bin at her shoe factory.

Papi shakes his head during our lively discussions. He says we will be home for my next birthday, but Abuela wags her finger at him and says that man proposes and God disposes.

More good things happened today. In school Srta. Reed called me to the front of the class to read aloud an essay she had assigned last week about the most important event that had happened in the past school year. I wrote about how I had learned English, so I did not expect to get a big red A on the corner of the first page because everybody else had written about more significant subjects. But Srta. Reed told the class that my essay was "a fine example of the correct use of grammar, proper development of ideas, and over-all good writing." Though she congratulated me, my knees shook when I read. My pronunciation is still so embarrassing. After class, Juan Carlos — the cute new boy who transferred here from New Jersey — asked me if I had seen the movie *The Dirty Dozen*, about a group of criminals who become heroes in a war. I had not, of course, but I was so thrilled that he had spoken to me that I arrived at social studies after the bell had rung.

Wednesday, 22nd of May

Well, who do you think came over this afternoon? Tommy. Ileana's Tommy. Remember him? And Ileana was at work! After he left, Abuela María kept nagging me to tell her who that *americano* was and what he wanted with Ileana. I kept my mouth shut, pretending to know nothing. My silence didn't help matters any, though. Abuela María still tattled to Mami.

Ileana says Tommy wants her to help him draw posters for a protest march. She is not sure what to do. One minute she wants to help because she likes Tommy and enjoys spending time with him. But the next minute she decides she doesn't have any time and is hurt that he is using her. He visits her only when he needs her to do something, but he doesn't bother to be nice at other times.

"If he really liked me," she said, "he wouldn't care if I had to go to a party with a chaperone. True love is about overcoming obstacles." She is sounding just like Mami.

Efraín announced to the family that he has signed up with the U.S. Marines. Tía Carmen nearly fainted when she found out, and Tío Pablo stood there like he had been frozen in place, mouth open. Only Papi went over to shake his hand. Efraín leaves in a few days for another state to begin a training program. I won't believe it until he actually goes. I think this is another one of his jokes.

Saturday, 25th of May

Jane's grandparents called this morning to talk to Papi. I don't know what they said on their end, but Papi was very polite and his English was surprisingly good. Later I overheard him tell Mami that the trip would take about ten days. We would visit Key West and Saint Augustine (the oldest city in the country), as well as Cape Canaveral and Tallahassee, the state capitol. We would spend some time in a couple of beach towns on the west coast of the state. It sounds so wonderful. Would it be selfish if I said a prayer for myself?

Monday, 27th of May

Americans celebrate Memorial Day in honor of those who have fought and died in war. It is a holiday where everybody flies the American flag. We don't have one, but Tío Pablo does and he displayed it from a pole on the side of the house. He also put a smaller Cuban flag beside it. I wonder if he feels a commitment to both or to only one. Do you stop loving your homeland if you live somewhere else and fly that country's flag? Must you surrender your memories to adapt to all the new demands of another life?

When I first started school, Srta. Reed had me memorize the Pledge of Allegiance. Remember that? I had to recite it to her by the end of the week. Though I was able to do it, I had no idea what the words said or what the whole pledge meant. It was like reciting gibberish. But now I know what those words stand for. When I put my hand over my heart, and when I declare my allegiance to those colors and to the republic they represent, I cannot help but wonder if this means I have forgotten my own country, my own flag, that first allegiance of my birth. This is very confusing, and I'm not sure I can even explain the division I sometimes feel inside my heart.

Wednesday, 29th of May

Efraín has left to train with the marines. How we miss him already! I am not exaggerating when I say that it seems as if the sun does not shine as bright and the house is quieter without him. Everyone walks around as if they are still asleep. Abuelo Tony complains his heart hurts, and Tía Carmen looks like she is twenty years older.

Efraín will probably be sent to Vietnam. That's

what Ileana says. Does that mean he will get killed there? Now I will pray for both Pepito and Efraín. I will pray in the morning, which I never do, and before bed, twice as long.

Friday, 31st of May

Every night this week, long after Ana Marı was asleep, I could hear Ileana sobbing into her pillow. At first it sounded like a strange breeze coming through the window. Then I thought it might be hiccups. Finally I realized what the sound was. When I asked her why she was crying, she said she was scared something horrible would happen to Efraín or Pepito because she was having nightmares about bombs and guns and babies being killed. I wish she hadn't told me because I do not want to think about it. I, too, worry about my brother and cousin.

Miami won't be the same without Efraín. I feel like I am alone trying to figure out the city and the people and the events that happen to me.

Saturday, 1st of June

Mrs. Henderson visited today. She spoke with Papi for a long time, explaining why this trip would be good for me. He didn't tell her either way about his decision, but her visit certainly helped.

Abuelo Tony also talked to Papi, and he was very, very convincing. He explained that sometimes we have to give up control to gain something more valuable. He also assured my parents that they should not worry about money because he had "a little grandfatherly sum" squirreled away for an event of this kind. "You have to allow your children to fly," Abuelo told Papi. I think my father may be ready to give in. I am so excited at the thought that I cannot fall asleep.

Monday, 3rd of June

We are waiting for a phone call from Cuba. Mami said she dreamed Pepito called during dinner, just as we were sitting to eat *tasajo*. (The shredded beef is one of his favorite meals.) Mami thinks the dream is a predictor of something, so now nobody can tie up the phone in the late afternoon or evening. Just in case Pepito calls.

I sure hope dreams come true, for my mother's sake.

Thursday, 6th of June

The whole country is sad. A man who was running for president, Robert F. Kennedy, was shot yesterday by a criminal, right there in a hotel where everybody could see. He died today. He is the brother of a president who was also assassinated, but that was before we had moved here. Again today, Abuelo said, "These are dark times." It is very depressing. On the television they showed Mr. Kennedy's wife crying. He has a whole bunch of children and they were crying, too. Now they are all orphaned.

I don't understand all this shooting. I don't understand the wars, either. Any war. I suppose the grown-ups think they have good reasons to fight each other, but if they do, I wish then they would leave my brother and cousin out of it. Jane told me she has a second cousin who refused to go to the war in Vietnam, so now he lives in Canada. Doing that is against the law, so he can never come back to see his family. In a way that situation is like my family's, but in reverse.

Pepito is in the Cuban army. He didn't want to be, but the government forced him anyway. This also means we don't know when we will see him next.

Friday, 7th of June

It is so hot now that Abuelo has decided we should do our exercise walks after dinner, when it's almost nightfall. Every day this week, though, it has rained on our plans. "That's summer in the tropics," Abuelo says. "Rain, rain, and more rain." We were finally able to walk today, and along the way we saw many beautiful plants and flowers as well as dragonflies and butterflies, grasshoppers, snails, slugs, and tiny aphids. Plenty of mosquitoes, too, unfortunately. We kept having to flap away the bugs.

We walked a little farther than on other days because Abuelo felt stronger and because the overcast sky kept away the worst of the heat. I am so glad we did, too. We got to see a house five blocks over that has a well-tended garden with a wide variety of species that Abuelo said made his heart sing. There was a beautiful shrimp plant and a golden shower tree, and marigolds, crossandra, and purple pentas in a flower bed bordering the house. Along a chain-link fence there were several kinds of flowering vines, too, but I can remember only one of the names — the jade vine because it had the most stunning aquamarine flowers. That wasn't all, though. In the far corner of the yard, a royal poinciana — we call it *framboyan*, which sounds like *flamboyant* — was in full bloom, and the red-orange flowers covered most of the branches. I have never seen such beautiful colors.

"Only God can make them like that," Abuelo told us.

To which Ana Mari responded, "If it is fine with God, then I want to be very rich when I grow up so I can live in a very big house with a very large garden. Then, Abuelo, you can come and help me plant it. I do not want to sweat, though, so we will plant only in the winter or when the sun is setting."

This made Abuelo laugh.

When we were returning home, I could tell Abuelo was tired. He had a hard time catching his breath. I kept insisting he rest, but he would not. He said his heart was still singing with the joy of the flowers and the colors, and that does not happen too often.

"When you are old," he added, "you take advantage of every happy moment."

Saturday, 8th of June

Ileana bought herself a record player with her own earnings. It is a small one we can put on the dresser in our bedroom, but it still cost a lot of money. She will not say how much, and Mami got very angry when she saw how she had wasted wages on something we do not need. But the money is, after all, hers. She earned it.

Ileana also bought several singles, and she has been playing them over and over all afternoon. Loud. By *loud*, I mean loud enough for the windows to rattle. About every fifteen minutes Mami knocks on the door and tells her to lower the volume. Ileana does. Then she waits about five minutes and slowly turns up the knob. She likes to play a singer named Bob Dylan all the time. If you listen closely to the words in his song, you understand how sad and angry he is. Ileana likes "A Hard Rain's A-Gonna Fall." I think he has a whiny voice, but Ileana says I don't know diddly-squat about music. What's diddly-squat? I have never heard that phrase in English. She also listens to the Rolling Stones and Jefferson Airplane. I like the Monkees. Their songs are happy and romantic. They are also very cute.

Mami has given up on any calls coming from Cuba. She says the dream was just that — a dream.

Sunday, 9th of June

Papi said yes. Yes, yes, yes! I am going on the car trip with Jane. Here I come, Key West, Saint Augustine, Cape Canaveral, and Tallahassee! I've started counting the hours. I'm already thinking about what I will pack. Jane says we will be staying at motels with pools, so I most certainly will pack my swimsuit.

We were spending the day at Crandon Park when Papi announced the good news. I had been moping all morning, remembering Efraín and how he had shown us the zoo and the roller rink last summer. But the idea of the trip perked me right up. Even Abuelo Tony was excited for me. "You will get more of an education by traveling than by sitting in a classroom," he said, and hugged me tight.

I've got to pinch myself to make sure I'm not dreaming.

Tuesday, 11th of June

I have lots of homework, and enough tests to bury me. I must write you about the photographs we received from Cuba, the ones Pepito promised. The person in the photographs hardly looks like Pepito. He is almost twice as tall as Abuelo Pancho, and his face is long and it ends in a square chin. He has serious, hard eyes. He looks thinner than I remember, too, but maybe it is just his uniform. I feel cheated. Instead of making me happy, the photographs gave me this ripping sensation in my chest. Of course, I didn't say anything to my parents. Why make a bad situation worse?

At least I have the trip to look forward to. Jane gave me some brochures from Cape Canaveral, and we saw pictures of Saint Augustine in a book in the school library.

Thursday, 13th of June

Hip, hip, hurrah for me. I received Best Mathematics Student award in a school ceremony for eighth graders. I was so surprised. Never in a million years did I expect this. Though my lowest mark in any examination or quiz was a 95, I still thought that Mrs. Boatwright did not like me because she would never smile at me and was always so strict. Last week the school sent home a note announcing the ceremony, but I did not think it was important and threw it away. Had I known, maybe Abuela or Abuelo could have come to school to see me receive the award.

As soon as Mami and Papi came home from work, I showed them the certificate. We immediately went to the shopping center to buy a frame for it and hung it on one of the bedroom walls. Papi said I inherited his way with numbers. Mami said that was fine as long as I didn't inherit his stubbornness. They laughed and kissed, and I decided that seeing them act silly was better than receiving the award itself.

Friday, 14th of June

Alina must attend summer school because she failed two classes. (She won't tell me which.) I think she is working too many hours. She should concentrate on school. Srta. Reed gave her some books to help improve her English. One is titled *Direct English Conversation for Foreign Students* by Robert J. Dixon.

Most of the lessons are vocabulary that I already know, so I promised to help her when I return from the car trip.

Sunday, 16th of June

Abuelo Tony died. He died. He's gone. My *abuelito.*

I write those words and still can't believe it. He had a heart attack. By the time the ambulance came, the paramedics could not revive him. Tío Pablo had to give Abuela medicine to calm her down because she was hysterical. She would not let the ambulance people take him or come near him. Now she has been sleeping all afternoon.

Oh, my *abuelito.* My dear, dear *abuelito.*

Later

No more tears, no more tears. I have cried myself out. I tried to be strong for Ana Mari because she has taken this very hard, but I got a horrible headache from holding in all my crying. So I went for a walk. Without telling any grown-up, either, which is a big no-no. I just forgot. I walked and walked and walked.

I was sweating rivers from so much walking. I went to all the places Abuelo and I would go during our exercises. I saw all the plants he pointed out to me and I tried to name them. Some I knew, others I had already forgotten. And the more I walked, and the farther I got from home, the more I was able to cry. I could let it all out without the worry of upsetting anybody. When I got to that pretty garden we saw a few days ago, I stood in front of the *framboyan* and cried even more. I am glad it was hot because no one was out in the streets. It would have been embarrassing if somebody had seen me.

I cannot believe I will never hear my Abuelo's voice again, or touch his hand, or see him walking beside me, panting because Ana Mari and I are moving too fast. Death is so final, so absolute, so unfair. I do not want to think about it.

Monday, 17th of June

I had never been to a funeral until this day. I hope I never have to go to another one. This one was a traditional Cuban wake. The funeral people had fixed Abuelo Tony up and dressed him in a fancy suit, so he could lie in an open casket. They put makeup on his face, too. When I knelt on the cushioned pew in front of the coffin to say a prayer, I looked at his fake smile and closed eyes and I knew for sure he was dead. Papi wanted me to kiss him, but I was afraid. He looked so . . . so unreal, like a wax doll. I did touch him, though, and he felt very hard and cold.

Efraín came home from boot camp this morning, but he must leave tomorrow afternoon. I hardly got to talk to him because the men mobbed him and asked him all kinds of questions. The funeral parlor was full of relatives and friends, all of them talking too loud. The old women sat in big chairs lining the room. Abuela was in the corner closest to Abuelo's body, sniffling and dabbing her eyes with a handkerchief. Every time someone new came up to her, she began to weep all over again. "Leave her alone," I wanted to scream. She kept complaining it was cold, and Tío Pablo gave her his jacket until Mami went home to get her a sweater. The air-conditioning was very, very cold. My fingernails were purple the whole time.

Everyone wore black, even Jane and Mrs. Henderson. Mr. and Mrs. F., from the craft store, came, and so did

Tommy and a few of Ileana's girlfriends, and Alina with her family. I was surprised how people kept coming in and out of the parlor with little plates of pastries or cups of *café* they had bought at a cafeteria down the block. To me all the commotion felt more like a party than anything else. I hated the noise and the relatives hugging me tight. I did not care for any of them. All I wanted was my Abuelo back. There were lots of flowers, too, so many that Ileana sneezed all afternoon. Mami gave her a special medicine to make her stop.

A priest came in the evening to recite the rosary. I just mumbled the words to go along. I wished he would go away, too, and he finally did, but not before coming to pat each of us on the head. I wanted to ask him why my Abuelo had died. Why didn't somebody else die, somebody mean, like Fidel Castro and those dictators in Russia and that man who killed Robert Kennedy and the other fellow who murdered Martin Luther King, Jr. Why?

We had to come home after the rosary because it was almost eleven o'clock. All the grown-ups will stay the night with Abuelo's body, then tomorrow after church we will bury him. I can't stop thinking about how Abuelo worried he would not ever see his homeland again. Maybe he knew something we didn't.

Tuesday, 18th of June

Early in the morning, before we left for the funeral parlor, I ran around the block collecting all the flowers I could see. I picked ixoras and marigolds and pentas and tiny lantanas and gardenias and appleblossom cassia and frangipani and allamanda and oleander. Back in the kitchen, all the names came to me suddenly, in a rush, as I wrapped their fragile stems in a moist napkin and then wrapped them again in foil.

At the parlor, when we went to say our final goodbyes to Abuelo, I put my special bouquet inside the casket. I am sure no one except Ana Mari understood what I was doing, and when she saw the beautiful flowers, all those bright colors against Abuelo's dark suit, she came over to hug me. Together we cried.

Now he is gone, and I miss him so much. So very much.

Friday 21st of June

It has rained for days. I feel like the heavens are crying with me. How I wish my *abuelo* were here. And my brother, too! And Efraín. It is so difficult to be away from people you love. I feel as if I cannot breathe, as if there is not enough fresh air to go around. I now know better than ever what Papi means by exile because in certain ways death is a form of exile. It is separation and finality and the ability to remember without the joy of touching or seeing or hearing.

Saturday, 22nd of June

It hit me: I am finally leaving on the trip tomorrow. I'm so excited.

Wednesday, 26th of June

We toured most of Saint Augustine today, though it was so hot we kept having to stop at different places to get a drink. This place reminds me a lot of Cuba, especially the Castillo de San Marcos at the edge of Matanzas Bay and Fort Matanzas, which is much smaller than the Castillo. We took lots of photographs. When I phoned my parents — I must call every evening — I felt a little homesick. That surprised me because I so much wanted to leave on this trip.

I'm having a great time with Jane and her grandparents. They insist I call them Gramps and Grannie, which I do, and they let us eat ice cream every day.

Sunday, 30th of June

I haven't forgotten you, but I have so little time. Today we motored around Lake Okeechobee with a fishing guide. This lake is so big it looks like an ocean. We also saw a lot of people in bus-like cars that Jane says are called recreational vehicles. People camp in them. I had never seen one before.

I'd write more if I weren't so exhausted.

Thursday, 4th of July

I'm back! It was the most fantastic vacation I have ever had. Jane's grandparents treated me so nicely. We swam in the ocean, we jumped from diving boards, we saw rocket ships, we sat on old Spanish cannons, we saw a sunset in Key West, we went fishing on a boat in Lake Okeechobee — oh, we did so many things that I will need a new diary to write them all.

Today is Independence Day, and it is celebrated with picnics and fireworks, but we did nothing except work around the house. I helped Mami refinish a dresser that she rescued from a trash pile on her way from work earlier in the week. "Amazing the usable things *los americanos* throw out," she says. "This is a country of such abundance." Her statement reminded me of those long lines we used to wait in for everything — soap, beans, rice, shoes, clothing. Abuelo Pancho used to say Cubans queued up for everything except death, and now poor Abuelo Pancho is still there in Cuba, standing in lines. When I told Mami what I was thinking, her eyes misted. She said it was not always like that in Cuba. Years ago, before the Communist revolution, when I was a little girl, you could buy most anything at any store if you had money. Now, even with money, there's nothing to buy.

In the late afternoon when it was a teensy bit cooler, Tía Carmen barbecued hot dogs and hamburgers. Then we went through some old photo albums that Abuela had brought from Cuba. We could not bring any of ours, so these photographs of our childhoods are very precious. Staring at them, I felt like I was spying on someone else's life, someone who looked like me but was existing in a parallel world of scalloped photo paper. It made me wonder what kind of life I might have had, the kind of life *all* my family would have had, if the Communists had not taken over our country. It would be very different if we had stayed behind. For one thing, I would not know any English. I would have never met Jane nor gone on that wonderful trip. Mami would not have learned to drive — at least not for a long time. Ileana would not have a job, and Papi would not have ever trained with those militias in the swamp. How strange that one event, one decision, can change so many parts of so many people's lives!

At night we saw the fireworks on television from the United States capital. It was beautiful to watch the night sky lighting up in what we knew were fantastic colors, even if it was only on a black-and-white screen and not in person. Next year, though, Tía Carmen has promised we will go to a park to see the fireworks and festivities. We will bring a blanket and lie on it and stare up at the darkness. (She always tries to be optimistic. It must be so hard for her to keep smiling while Efraín is away.)

"The colors of the fireworks in the night look like exploding flowers," she explained. "You will see what I mean next year."

So what do you think Papi said to Tía Carmen? One guess. That's right. He said, "Next year we'll be in Cuba." And he said, too, that instead of staring into the dark sky, we will be taking an evening swim in Guanabo. I wish I could believe him.

My Personal Exodus
Ana Veciana-Suarez

My father was a comptroller of a national bank in Havana and my mother a housewife when, on New Year's Eve of 1958, Cuban leader Fidel Castro overthrew the Fulgencio Batista government. I was just two years old, and now have few memories of those times except for blurry images of our front porch and the wrought-iron gate that led to it. But this I do know: Like many of their friends and neighbors, my parents welcomed the change and never suspected that the much-awaited revolution would soon turn Communist.

As the new Castro government confiscated private property, however, and firing squads exacted revenge on counterrevolutionaries, thousands of families left all their possessions behind in hopes of finding a temporary haven in the United States. Most settled in Miami, where the exile community became very politically active. Thousands of exiles joined anti-Castro groups, many of them subsidized by the American government. In April of 1961 more than 1,400 men, who had trained in Central America under the auspices of the United States, launched an unsuccessful attack on Cuba at the Bay of Pigs.

My family was still in Cuba during the Bay of Pigs invasion, and it wasn't until May 1961 that my mother was able to leave with my brother and sister and me for Spain. (A younger brother and sister would be born later in exile.) My father remained on the island, fighting in the underground. In October of that year he fled the island with my grandmother and a group of men on a fourteen-foot boat. They were rescued by the U.S. Coast Guard, and we were reunited in New York a month later. Eventually we joined the growing Cuban community in Miami. My parents found jobs, we children were registered in school, and, along with both sets of grandparents, we went about the business of preparing to return to Cuba. Everyone thought the stay in the United States would be temporary.

But the exodus of Cubans to Miami continued, in

spurts and, by air and boat, for decades. Perhaps the most poignant departures took place from 1960 to 1962, through Operation Pedro Pan, a program to get children off of the island when their parents had not been granted permission to leave immediately with them. About 14,000 Cuban children fled Cuba alone. Many didn't see their parents for years and lived in foster homes and orphanages across the country. I have several friends and relatives who arrived in the United States under this program. Some came with older siblings, but others traveled alone, and it was an experience that rushed them out of childhood and into youthful responsibility.

The next big migration of Cuban exiles began in 1965, when Castro opened the port of Camarioca to anyone who wanted to leave the country. In less than a month, between October 10 and November 15, more than 6,000 fled in all manner of boats, most of them supplied by relatives already in Miami. It was a dangerous journey, but one that many had taken across the Straits of Florida before 1965 and still make now in homemade rafts, inner tubes, and tiny fishing boats.

I was almost nine years old when Camarioca opened and clearly remember how my parents desperately searched for a boat captain who would bring my mother's sister and her children to the United States. (Her husband was a political prisoner.) Castro, however, closed the port before my aunt was able to leave. About two years later her family boarded a Freedom Flight to Miami. Started in December 1965, this airlift was made possible because of negotiations between the U.S. and Cuban governments after the closing of Camarioca. By the time the twice-a-day flights ended in April 1973, more than 260,560 refugees like Yara García and my aunt had come to the United States.

The exiles' presence changed Miami. The same year the Freedom Flights stopped, the county commission proclaimed Dade a bilingual and bicultural county, and Maurice Ferre, born in Puerto Rico, became Miami's first Latin mayor. Though migration from the island slowed in the late 1970s, the United States and Cuba opened Diplomatic Interests Sections in each other's capitals in 1977. In 1978 the Cuban government also began talking with Cuban exiles to negotiate the release of political prisoners. By November 1979, 3,900 political prisoners had been freed. Most settled in Miami, among them my uncle, who was able to be reunited with his family after serving almost twenty years in prison.

Charter flights bearing exiles back to the island also began in January 1979, the first time refugees could visit their homeland since 1961. Though I have never been back, several of my relatives have, including my younger sister born in the United States. This ability to travel to and from the island, however, did little to stop the migration of Cubans who wanted to leave for a better life in the United States. In April 1980, after 10,000 Cubans hoping for freedom flooded the embassy of Peru in Havana, Castro opened the port of Mariel to any exiles who wanted to rescue relatives. Like the Camarioca boat lift fifteen years earlier, but on a much larger scale, exiles' boats and yachts invaded the Cuban coastline. When Mariel closed in September, more than 120,000 refugees had left the island. As many as 100,000 settled in Miami, including one of my great aunts and several of my cousins.

With each wave of refugees, Miami became increasingly Hispanic. Cuban political power grew. During and after the Mariel boat lift, Hispanics constituted a majority on the Miami City Commission, and the

1980s witnessed many political firsts as Cuban-born politicians were elected mayors, school board representatives, and county commissioners. At that time several cities in south Florida — Hialeah, Miami, and Miami Beach — already had or were close to having a Hispanic majority.

One of the most recent — and most dangerous — exoduses from Cuba occurred during the summer of 1994, when tens of thousands of Cubans took to the sea in all manner of floating devices. During a thirty-seven-day period, about 32,000 survived the journey across the Straits of Florida, but countless others died at sea. Many rafts, floating like corks adrift in the large ocean, were found eerily empty by the U.S. Coast Guard and private Brothers to the Rescue planes. Although the United States continues to welcome Cubans fleeing the Castro regime, its immigration laws are stricter now, and many Cubans who have recently attempted to flee to this country have been deported back to the island.

Exiles who, like Yara's father and my own family, expected to return to their homeland in a few months ended up making Miami home. Many who had relocated to cities in the north in the 1960s and 1970s —

as had my uncles, aunts, and cousins — eventually returned to the warmer climate of Florida. With freedom on our side, we built hospitals, shopping centers, schools, and housing developments. We went on to become teachers, doctors, lawyers, mechanics, developers, politicians, journalists, actresses, and beauty pageant queens.

Now, more than forty years after the first wave of Cubans to the United States, in an act of gratitude the exile community is raising funds for a complete multi-million-dollar transformation of El Refugio — the downtown Freedom Tower that housed the Cuban Refugee Emergency Center, where about 450,000 exiles, like Yara's family and my own, received generous emergency help from the U.S. government from 1962 to 1974. The Freedom Tower will serve as an interactive museum, research center, and library chronicling the Cuban exile experience in south Florida.

Acknowledgments

I would like to thank Luis Orta and Guillermo "Willy" Aguilar for their many stories of Cuba, particularly those they shared with me about *La Escuela al Campo*. Thank you also to Carolina Hospital for her advice and to my parents, Sira and Antonio Veciana, who refreshened my memory of our early years in this wonderful country.